The
Timekeeper's
Daughter

DALE PESKIN

PAGE PUBLISHING, INC.
Conneaut Lake, PA

First originally published by Page Publishing 2020

ISBN 978-1-64584-665-9 (pbk)
ISBN 978-1-64584-666-6 (digital)

Printed in the United States of America

For Mary, Amanda, my mother and the women
who have guided me across time.

Such a small murder so long ago should be forgiven in a place such as Youngstown—unless you understand the importance of keeping time.

The End and the Beginning of Imagination

The ambush came without warning. Five thousand steelworkers in Youngstown, Ohio, lost their livelihoods on Monday, September 19, 1977, when the Youngstown Sheet & Tube Co. announced the immediate closing of its Campbell Works steel plant. It was, at the time, the single largest mass elimination of jobs in the nation's history. It took just a few minutes for an entire city to become inconsequential.

In all, 60,000 workers in Youngstown were displaced in the wave of plant closings that followed. The betrayal of community purpose in American life was so stunning that Bruce Springsteen wrote a song about it. He called it "Youngstown."

More than 300,000 steel jobs were lost throughout the Rust Belt following the day known as Black Monday. It was the day industrial America died.

* * *

The seeds of decline were sown in the 1970s. It was called the "Me Decade," but the seventies were actually more about tumult. All the certainties of the American experience began to crumble. The US lost a war in Vietnam and its moral authority in the world. Iran held Americans hostage as part of a fundamentalist religious revolution that spread globally. An oil embargo by Arab petroleum-producing countries forced Americans to queue their vehicles around filling stations in hopes of pumping a few gallons of available gasoline. Factories became obsolete, jobs endangered. The American Dream evolved into a national nightmare as high mortgage rates put home ownership out of reach for almost every American.

That was only the beginning. The decade brought a global recession and a profound social struggle. America began a restructuring that took it from a nation committed to shared prosperity to one of tribalism and increasing class polarization.

Marginalized Americans lead by women and blacks pressed their fight for equality. A new Right mobilized in defense of political conservatism and traditional family roles. The conduct of President Richard Nixon undermined many people's faith in the American government, an omen for administrations to come. By the end of the decade, these divisions and disappointments had set a divisive and pessimistic course for the nation. The great American decline had started.

* * *

The course was reset with a new invention. It was introduced in the January 1975 issue of *Popular Electronics*. The first personal computer, the MITS Altair 8800, came in a kit. There were no computer or electronic stores to buy one. For $439, it included assembly instructions, a metal case, a power supply, and all the boards and components required to build it. It took hours of careful soldering and intricate assembly. Only true hackers undertook the task, and they weren't certain the gizmo would work.

It did work. Waves of technological advancement followed: floppy discs for storing and moving data; a system known as Ethernet for connecting computer systems to form a local communications network; and applications for business calculations, spreadsheets and word processing. Then came personal photography and video. Childhood friends Bill Gates and Paul Allen formed a company called Microsoft to provide software for the Altair 880. With a few friends in his parents' garage, college dropout Steve Jobs poached an experimental design from Xerox and created a home computer that could be operated intuitively. He called the company "Apple," urging the willing to excuse accepted grammar and "think different."

They did think different. One million personal computers were sold by the end of the decade, somewhat more than the five that the chairman of IBM said the world needed. Other businesses began to use the technology. Information was democratized. Creative destruction forced every institution and every person to reimagine how to exist. Work, life, communications, and all the relationships that connected people to each other were reordered as enabling technology shifted power to the individual.

Many saw the computer revolution as an opportunity to build a society that amended the failures of the physical world, a place where idealistic young men and women thought they could redesign the rules of society. It was the end and the beginning of imagination all at the same time.

PART ONE

INTO THE FOG

INTO THE FOG

Something.

An unsettling thought woke the Timekeeper from a restless sleep. Something was amiss. He sensed that the order of things had been disrupted. It was a feeling, nothing that could be reconciled quickly. And that made it all the more disturbing.

Something.

The uneasiness persisted. A premonition? Intuition about the unforeseen? A hunch? Or lingering gas from last night's greasy pizza?

Something.

Hoping to identify the distraction that consumed him, the Timekeeper decided to follow his routine rigorously. Any exception to it might yield a clue that could explain his apprehension. He loaded coffee grounds into a Mr. Coffee brew basket, filled the carafe with tap water, and then poured it into a plastic filtration system. Forgetting to insert the paper filter, he watched the coffeemaker merely rinse, rather than brew, the beans, filling the carafe with coffee-flavored water.

Next, he pulled a frying pan from the cupboard and an egg carton from the fridge. An egg broke in his hand before he could scramble it in the pan. The golden yolk soaked into the white cuff of his long-sleeved shirt.

Exacting in every facet of his life, the Timekeeper couldn't remember ever torturing coffee or mishandling a simple egg. Routine broken, he cleaned the mess as his uncertainty mounted.

Something.

The Timekeeper dressed by ritual. He hung his timepiece from the fob attached to his belt, then slipped it into the watch pocket of his Dickies work pants. On his other hip, he hung a retractable, industrial-strength key chain pulling a crowded set of keys. Still unsettled, a reassuring thought crossed his mind. Reaching into the neck of his shirt, he lifted a long chain over his head. A simple wooden cross—two rectangular blocks of wood connected by a simple screw to form the cross—dangled from the chain.

Then came a premonition that something else, something more serious, would go wrong. He removed the chain and carefully looped it around the top corner of the mirror that hung in the hallway between the two bedrooms of the cottage.

In the name of the father.

The words came to him as if a prayer. The meaning would be clear to the only person who understood.

The Timekeeper had long abandoned the teachings of his strict spiritual upbringing in a church in Tennessee. He scoffed at justifying religion by faith alone, questioned the grace of God, and rejected predetermination, the most absurd tenet of Presbyterian doctrine. He had become an enthusiastic agnostic, a mortal who believed the concept of a supreme celestial dictator was a universal con perpetrated through time. He believed the world's religions were founded in fear with the arrogant manipulating the gullible with a shallow promise of salvation for a price. The best that sinners could expect was shelter from the storm. Or so he was reminded by his precocious daughter, a devotee of the poet-prophet Robert Allen Zimmerman. Sing not of hymns when you can listen to Dylan.

In the name of the father.

Father, lowercase "f." The Timekeeper wasn't praying; he was leaving a clue. An object of no religious significance was set in an obvious place to misdirect any trespasser who'd trespass against the father and daughter.

Moving out of the hallway, the Timekeeper turned to the kitchen and poured the swill from the Mr. Coffee into a silver bullet thermos. Then he set out for work.

Placing the thermos next to his hard hat in the front seat, the Timekeeper climbed into the gold Cutlass coupe. It was a 1976 model with waterfall-split grilles and rectangular headlights. The Oldsmobile packed a Rocket V8 engine, 455 cubic inches that when floored, would set you back in your seat and propel you into the next dimension—a rare fantasy the Timekeeper allowed himself. Truth was he felt powerful and stylish in America's best-selling car. And it was made in the US, not Japan, with *our* steel. He pulled away from his isolated cottage on Mosquito Lake and headed toward the Brier Hill Works, seventeen miles south.

Something.

Still troubled and confused, the Timekeeper approached the massive plants along the Mahoning River without the recollection of driving there. The sleepless night, the ruined coffee, the broken egg, the shattered routine, and the premonition about the chain—he was being presented clues. He meant to unravel them.

Everything changes. People age and die. Cultures crumble. The stars burn out. The gradual dispersal of energy is evidence of an irreversible arrow of time, the quantum effect known as entanglement.

The Timekeeper structured his life around this fundamental theorem of linear time. He was neither physicist nor philosopher, merely the manager of a steel mill nearing the end of its time. All operations and all the lives intertwined among them depended on timing: the coke mill that cooks coal into a fuel for the blast furnaces; the smelting furnaces that blast iron ore, coke, and limestone into liquid iron; the oxygen furnaces that convert iron into steel; the hot strip mills that shape the steel into sheets, coils, bars, and plates; the pickling and annealing mills that remove impurities; and the rail and trucking yards that distributed steel throughout an industrialized nation.

One process leads to another. If the timing is off, the chemistry fails, the assembly line breaks, and plants close. Jobs are lost, businesses fail, and towns are destroyed. Time and place devolve into a state of uniform desolation. It was up to the Timekeeper to maintain equilibrium.

While the Timekeeper achieved balance by putting events and processes in their proper order, he was not convinced his methodology was correct. But it was practical. People are not conditioned to see events as unconnected and inexplicable. Nor could any organization accept capitalism and its entrenched flow of commerce over time as an illusion. The idea that past, present, and future are equally real and that the world is a process of ceaseless change was too disruptive for pedestrian thinkers. Flux and decay would disrupt society and its value systems so completely that, the Timekeeper believed, humanity would devolve into chaos.

So he stood for order: A-theory. If time were an illusion, he would wait for the quantum evidence to reset it.

As the Timekeeper considered his options, the Cutlass drove itself along a familiar course. Unbeknownst to its preoccupied driver, it passed the turnoff to the north gate of the Brier Hill Works. A mile of steel mills passed before the Timekeeper recognized his mistake. For years, he regularly turned off the highway at the road leading to the north gate.

Thousands of right turns into the plant without thinking. It's my routine. Today, I drive by. What am I thinking? What is happening?

The question brought decisions. Turn around? Proceed to the south gate? Acknowledge that something was seriously amiss and return home?

Time may bend back, but not today.

The Timekeeper proceeded to the south gate, another mile down the highway. At the base of Brier Hill, the road dipped sharply to the valley along the Mahoning River. The Cutlass approached a road sign that read "Fog Area."

With the river nearby, water droplets could have created the atmospheric condition that resulted in the low-lying cloud impairing visibility. But the stench of rotten eggs—sulfur—betrayed the cause. It was smoke from the coke plant, a thick and noxious goo of cloudy chemicals, gases, and carcinogens expelled from the plant. The smelly waste from the smelting process made it nearly impossible to follow the road into the south gate.

The Timekeeper made a mental note to find Einer Arnesson, aka Robin Hood. The slight Norwegian millwright would climb a ladder on the side of an adjacent smokestack to a parapet overlooking the coke plant's odious stack. Drawing an arrow from his quiver, Robin Hood would strike a flint to ignite the tip of the arrow. Setting his bow at the perfect arc, he'd shoot a flaming arrow into the gaseous waste spewing from the offending smokestack. The flame would ignite the gas above the smokestack, and the cloud would dissipate. Visibility would turn clear for the arrival of workers for the seven-to-three shift.

But *something* would not burn off. Dawn approached. Foreboding became more palpable as if *something* was about to happen. The gold Cutlass turned into the foggy half-light of the morning.

THE STIFF SHIFT

The stiff shift wasn't exactly the kind of assignment Jordan Maier had in mind. The reporter had returned to Youngstown to make his mark. Not that *The Youngstown Examiner* lived up to the estimable objective of its name. No one in Youngstown, nor the entire institution of journalism, for that matter, could recall *The Examiner* examining anything other than ways to entice more advertisers.

But like a generation of journalists inspired by Woodward and Bernstein, Maier came home to practice a craft that could expose power, corruption, and injustice. His hometown was the right place to start.

The editors at *The Examiner* humored Maier's ambition by assigning him to an empty newsroom in desolate downtown Youngstown on a Sunday night. There could be no more depressing place to enlighten the world than from a dingy room of industrial-strength steel desks, stacked papers, rotary phones, metal headsets, and console-sized computers tethered to power poles dangling from the ceiling. A few weeks on the stiff shift would disabuse the hotshot reporter of self-importance, reminding him that he was back in Youngstown and wouldn't be reporting for *The New York Times* any time soon.

The shift brought a charm of its own. The principal assignment: call funeral homes and gather information to write obituaries for the next day's editions. *The Examiner's* editors had established rigid rules for announcing that so-and-so was dead to a readership that didn't care that so-and-so was, for a time, alive. The rules were based on time. Newspaper time. *The Examiner* imposed a penalty on any soul discourteous enough to die after deadline.

For example, if poor George Kudzma of Struthers died before the afternoon newspaper's 10:00 a.m. deadline, his obituary would read "George Kudzma, 73, of Struthers, died at St. Elizabeth Hospital Tuesday…"

But if George managed his death inconveniently—after 10:00 a.m.—his obit would start with his final send-off: "Funeral services will be held at 2:00 p.m. Wednesday at Holy Trinity Roman Catholic Church for George Kudzma, 73, of Struthers, who died…"

One or the other, no embellishment. No calls to the family. No life stories. No unpleasant details about death. Just the necessary facts followed by survivors, visitation hours at the funeral home, church, time of funeral services, and where to make contributions in the deceased's name. Must get these right at all costs. Timing is everything.

Like death, the obituary was Youngstown's great equalizer. It brought order to Youngstown's bizarre caste system. Steelworker or steel baron, merchant or mobster, corrupt cop or political hack—die on time and get your due. Just do it before 10:00 a.m. if you value your name over your funeral.

Maier regarded the rules as arcane, the formula beneath his talents. He believed there was a unique story in every life. The reporter's craft was to discover the story and write it meaningfully. Seeking such a story, he began to work through the call list of funeral homes, speaking to morticians-in-training who, like him, had been assigned to the funeral home version of *The Examiner*'s stiff shift. An hour into the calls, one of the ghouls called him back.

"It's Julian Kaszlowski from Simcheck & Sons Funeral Home. I've got a body you might be interested in."

The night-shift embalmer worried if he was doing the right thing by calling the newspaper. He proceeded cautiously.

"The body came in Friday. Industrial accident, they said."

"Who said?" Maier asked.

"Security at Youngstown Steel. They brought him in."

"No ambulance?"

"Ambulance? Ah…yeah, I think so."

"How about the sheriff's office?"

"No, nothing like that."

"Then, like what?"

"Like nothing. It happens out here."

Maier didn't want to challenge the embalmer beyond the knowledge of his everyday routine.

"Okay," he said. "Where did he die?"

"I guess it was inside the mill. They called an ambulance and sent him over here, put him on my table."

"Who's 'they?'"

"Don't know. Wasn't here."

"How did he die?"

"He fell, but I don't think that killed him."

"How's that?"

"I think it was asphyxia. The guy breathed in some bad stuff, probably fumes, depleted his oxygen. I could tell when I was embalming the body."

"Embalming? So much for evidence."

Kaszlowski was defensive now. "Evidence? Evidence of what? I'm just doing my job. They bring them in, and I embalm them. That's all."

"I was just wondering why there wasn't a report or an investigation," Maier asked, trying to rebuild trust with the night-shift embalmer. "Anyone call the coroner?"

"I don't think so."

"That's odd."

"I thought so too. That's why I called."

"What can you tell me?"

"Just the basics for the obituary."

"Okay. Go ahead."

"Lou Epperson, fifty-six, a steelworker at the Brier Hill Works. That's l-o-u, not Lewis. Address: 3996 Lake Shore Drive, Cortland. You got that?"

Maier went silent.

"You know where that is?" the embalmer asked.

"I know where it is," Maier said solemnly. "Anything else?"

"Yeah. Seems he has a daughter. But I don't know where she is or how to get in touch."

"I do," said Maier.

"Am I going to get in trouble?" the embalmer asked sheepishly.

Not nearly as much as I am, Jordan Maier thought as he hung up the phone.

THE CRUCIBLE

LouAnn Epperson was emerging from hell, not that she believed in such a place. The meaning of the handcrafted cross hanging from the hallway mirror of her father's cottage held no religious significance. Rather, it was a talisman shared by father and daughter, an object from which only the two of them could discern purpose and meaning.

In the midst of a room she barely recognized as the parlor, she sat cross-legged on the floor, sobbing.

Who would do such a thing?

It was more than she could bear. First, the awful call she received in the lab at Caltech. Then the five-hour red-eye from LAX to O'Hare followed by the prop flight that bounced between Chicago and Cleveland. Then a two-hour, $200 cab ride to Simcheck & Sons Funeral Home in Cortland where she was greeted by the vampire, Count Simcheck. Then the worst of it all—the count showing her to the viewing room where her father was laid out in a JCPenney suit.

"He looks natural, at peace. Don't you think?" the count said.

Natural? At peace? My father's dead, you ghoul. He's leaving this world in JCPenney.

"We had to take a few liberties, but everything has been taken care of."

Overwrought, LouAnn could barely form words. She managed only three: "Liberties? By whom?"

"The company, of course. Youngstown Steel. Mr. Landry was very agreeable. He said to see to everything, even the suit."

"Landry was here?"

"Of course, my dear. He was very concerned."

She wanted to ask how her father died, but it came out "Could you take me home?"

"Of course, my dear. What would you like me to do with the body?"

Unprepared for the question, LouAnn forgot to ask an equally important one: How did my father die? Ten minutes later, she walked into the unrecognizable interior of her father's cottage, sat on the floor, and began to sob uncontrollably.

When her breath returned, she remembered that she hadn't used her key to enter the cottage. The door was open. Nothing else was as it should have been. Drawers were pulled out of her father's roll-top desk, their contents emptied on the floor. Beds were overturned. Dressers were cleaned out. Clothes were pulled from closets. Books were removed from shelves. Family photos were thrown on the floor. The family's prized collection of home movies and Hollywood films were strewn about the parlor. Then she noticed that the camera and movie player that her father brought back from Japan were missing.

Only the chain hanging from the mirror had not been touched. The intruders had no way of understanding its intended purpose. They could not know that it had been placed there for LouAnn, a message that only she would understand.

LouAnn removed the chain from the mirror, holding the simple, homemade cross in her hand. She knew immediately what to do. She reached in her blouse and pulled out a companion cross, a replica of the one her father left behind. With a slight twist, she turned the horizontal block until it was parallel with the vertical one. Then she slid the block upward along a channel that had been cut into it.

Taking her father's cross, she twisted it at the connecting screw at the center of the cross. A small stud extended from the back of the cross. LouAnn inserted the stud side of her father's cross into the channel on her cross. She twisted it precisely, a half turn. A single block was formed: a crude yet ingenious, handmade key.

LouAnn went to her bedroom, stooping at the dollhouse, a replica of the cottage that her father made for her seventh birthday. Like the chain on the mirror, the dollhouse had not been violated. Apparently, the intruders weren't interested in a child's treasure.

LouAnn pulled a miniature carpet from her room in the dollhouse and then removed a small section of the floor. Part of the subfloor was cut out. LouAnn positioned the key made from the two crosses into the empty spaces of the subfloor—a lock. The key fit precisely in the lock. She turned a raised portion of the key in the mechanism. A small drawer opened from the basement chamber of the dollhouse. LouAnn solved the puzzle; she could claim her prize.

This was how LouAnn received prizes and discovered messages from her father. The cherished ritual between father and daughter was part of their bond over time. Now the father had left his daughter a final prize, a final message: oddly, a video cassette from their trip to Japan, LouAnn's college graduation gift. The words *Japan, 1971* were written on the shell of the cassette. Without the Japanese movie player that had been removed from the cottage, there was no way to play the video.

"I'm not ready for this," she said aloud.

"It's time," came an answer in her head.

"Daddy?

"It's time, LouAnn."

"Daddy, I don't know what to do."

"Do what you were born to do, my amazing girl."

Then the Timekeeper's voice was gone.

As if on cue, a phone rang. *Who knows this number? Who knows about the enchanted Epperson cottage?* Spooked by the unexpected call, LouAnn felt suddenly exposed, as if she was being watched.

The phone in the cottage sat on a table in the short hallway between her room and her father's. It was situated under the mirror from where the chain with a wooden cross was hung—a clue known only to the father and daughter. Rather than answer the call, LouAnn's instinct was to protect their secret and hide her private discovery. She put the cassette back into the secret drawer of the dollhouse, closed it, and removed the father-daughter key. Hiding the secret lock, she carefully replaced the flooring in the dollhouse, pulled the miniature rug over the secret lock, and covered the rug with miniature furniture. By the time she reached the phone, it had stopped ringing. LouAnn was relieved by the solitary grief.

Privacy is undervalued.

The phone rang again. Now in full denial, she again hesitated to answer. But then a more powerful instinct took hold, the one that defined her as a scientist: the need to know. Information, no matter how painful, might somehow explain an awful event. *What have I missed?*

With the death of her father, LouAnn had become the central player in a crucible, the unwitting protagonist in a trial beyond her understanding. In her grief, she was compelled to understand the dark, interrelated stories that would unfold.

LouAnn approached her destiny with initial caution. Her first obligation was to protect the Epperson compact from anyone seeking to damage it. She untwisted the father-daughter key, returning it into two separate wooden crosses. With the ringing phone testing her nerves and her patience, she draped one cross from the corner of the hallway mirror as her father did.

The ringing continued. *Why won't they stop?* LouAnn picked up the receiver just as the persistent caller was about to give up. She recognized the voice immediately.

"Is that you Billy Pilgrim?" she asked. "Where have you been?"

UNSTUCK IN TIME

Is that you, Billy Pilgrim? Where have you been?

LouAnn Epperson's questions both comforted and jarred Jordan Maier. It had been seven years since the college friends had spoken. He wasn't sure how to answer.

"I'm here, LouAnn. You okay?"

"Define okay."

LouAnn had been back home for just a few hours. Her life had been turned upside down. She was distraught; that was to be expected. But there was more in her voice, the confusing echo of an unresolved relationship.

Is that you, Billy Pilgrim?

It was code. As college students, LouAnn and Jordan adopted Vonnegut's *Slaughterhouse Five* as a metaphor for their current existence. Jordan took the persona of Billy Pilgrim, the complacent, time-traveling, anti-war hero who was the book's protagonist. He was the editor of the college newspaper when students nationwide were protesting the Vietnam War. LouAnn was an engineering student smarter than anyone on campus, including faculty in any department.

Where have you been?

Jordan recalled the closing passage in the novel they called "S5," a satire about war and time travel that resonated with a generation and passionately with Jordan and LouAnn: "I have become unstuck in time."

That's what Jordan wanted to say, but it was too clever for his reunion with LouAnn, a kindred spirit who deserted him. A little too cruel too.

Is that you, Billy Pilgrim? Where are you?

An expectation—no, a demand—that he be there for her, no matter the time, no matter the place. Seven years and not a word. Until now.

"I'm on my way." Jordan meant the words to be reassuring. But they came out surprising chilly.

"Just get here soon, will you?"

LouAnn sounded sorrowful now. Separated by years, the feelings between her and Jordan were suddenly rekindled. The connections that were the core of their relationship—their admiration for each other, the shared college experiences, their mutual dependency, and the searing sexual tension—streamed back.

"Fast as I can travel through time," Billy Pilgrim promised.

Jordan checked out an X Car from the advertising department: an orange Chevy Nova with the words *The Examiner* painted in large black letters on the sides. The cars were used during the day by the advertising and circulation departments to deliver tear sheets to advertisers or undelivered papers to subscribers. After business hours, the news department used the vehicles to travel to assignments. Reporters regarded the fleet of Xcars as their personal Batmobiles, chariots that showcased their superpowers around Youngstown. Throughout the rest of the city, the vehicles were regarded as motorized pumpkins.

The reporter steered his pumpkin toward the Mahoning River, picking up the road that followed the river northwest from downtown. The steel mills hugged the river from downtown to the city limits, the hulking plants rising along the factory sewer that was formerly a tributary. From the road, the silhouettes of the plants merged into the dark storm clouds that settled over the river valley.

At Division Street, a winding crevice that passed between the coke plant and blast furnace at the south gate of the Brier Hill Works, Jordan recalled his first thought at the plant's gate: *Hell with the lid off.*

It was Lou Epperson who changed his perspective. To Lou, the Brier Hill Works was a dramatic chemistry project where ore, coke, and limestone were blasted into liquid metal in a chimneylike furnace. It was a light show where liquid steel was poured into ingots and slabs that flashed through rolling mills. It was an artist studio where master craftsmen forged and shaped the hot steel with hammers or presses, or extruded it to give it its desired shape.

Lou Epperson made steelmaking an epic poem. With Lou as his guide, Jordan discovered the intricate wonders of steelmaking during two memorable summers of his college years.

Lou's sudden death in the Brier Hill Works didn't make sense. He knew every inch of the plant, every process, and every accident waiting to happen. He calculated all the equations that put men in harm's way. He knew how to walk the gauntlet, how to avoid danger in a dangerous place. There was no scenario in which Lou Epperson could die accidentally in his steel mill.

Jordan Maier regarded the storm clouds hanging over the Mahoning as ominous. If he had never met LouAnn Epperson or her father, he would have long ago abandoned Youngstown and a mediocre career at a mill-town newspaper. Lou Epperson brought him to the mills. Jordan met LouAnn during his freshman year at Youngstown State. That summer, he was hired for a summer job at the Brier Hill Works. LouAnn needed only to ask her father.

As he drove the Xcar past the Brier Hill Works, Jordan spotted the Bendover Building near the far gate. His memory of the building was vivid. It was where he stood in line with hundreds of Youngstown boys, all clutching the only résumé that was required for a job as a millwright: a driver's license showing that they were at least eighteen. Dressed only in their undershorts and T-shirts, the boys moved army-style from one station to the next as they were evaluated for the job of millwright. At the final station, a company doctor asked Jordan to drop his shorts and bend over. As he rose without his dignity in the Bendover Building, he was pronounced fit to work at Youngstown Steel.

THE TIMEKEEPER'S DAUGHTER

Jordan was assigned a coveted job in the shipping department, perhaps the safest job in the mill for a student whose idea of hard work was pressing keys on a typewriter. On his first day of work, Lou Epperson introduced himself.

"So you are the young man that my daughter speaks so highly of," he said, sizing Jordan up. "You will come to no harm here. You will wear a hard hat and steel-toed boots at all times. You will wear gloves. You will keep them clear from grappling hooks that snap fingers off in a heartbeat. Reporters need fingers to type. They also need hearts. You will pay attention at all times. You will learn everything you can. We shall speak of these things at other times."

Working summers in the mill, the college student collected stories about the steelworkers who committed their lives—and those of their families—to a hard yet satisfying existence. He learned from Lou how to translate it into a poem about survival and fate. Time ran through it. Lou was its keeper.

As the orange Xcar pulled into Continuum, the Epperson cottage on Mosquito Lake, all the memories rushed back. Billy Pilgrim became unstuck in time.

ONE TIME, ONE MEETING

LouAnn Epperson's graduation party was not for the unimaginative. Lou and LouAnn draped a huge banner between two trees at their cottage on Mosquito Lake. Four Japanese characters on the banner declared "*ichi-go ichi-e*," an idiom for "one time, one meeting."

The banner intended to remind guests that many meetings in life are not repeated. Even when the same group of people can get together again, a celebration may never be replicated. Each moment is always once in a lifetime.

The few guests who actually came to the graduation party found humor in the theme. They were greeted by the Japanese Eppersons. Lou wore a samurai's kimono over his work wear. The getup looked particularly ridiculous with the yellow Youngstown Steel hard hat that was always on his head. On the other hand, LouAnn was a vision. She wore an embroidered silk kimono over nothing of consequence underneath.

Beyond the banner, the Eppersons installed a large *chabudai*, the short-legged table used in traditional Japanese homes. Guests removed their shoes and slid onto tatami mats placed on the grass around the table. The Eppersons then conducted *chakai*, the traditional "way of tea" ceremony, to entertain their guests.

Only two steelworkers from Lou's crew showed: the overhead crane operator, Jonny Mann, and the hillbilly handyman, Hoppy Crawford. They were joined by two members of the faculty at Youngstown State University, both doctors of engineering whose combined knowledge was eclipsed by the prodigy known as LouAnn

Epperson. The fifth guest was Jordan Maier, the only classmate of LouAnn's who made the twenty-five-mile trip from the YSU campus. LouAnn rather liked the turnout.

Jordan was the guest that mattered. Pouring green tea into a tiny cup, she bowed, bringing her lips to his ear. "Tonight, I am geisha," she whispered seductively.

After the tea party, the guests moved to the firepit that was situated under a protected canopy of oak trees near the lake. There, joints of marijuana were shared freely among the celebrants. After repeated tokes, the thoroughly stoned host rose to tell a story:

"One day, a young Buddhist on his journey home came to the banks of a wide river..." Lou preached to accompanying groans. "Staring hopelessly at the great obstacle in front of him, he pondered for hours on just how to cross such a wide barrier. Just as he was about to give up his pursuit to continue his journey he saw a great teacher on the other side of the river.

"The young Buddhist yells over to the teacher, 'Oh wise one, can you tell me how to get to the other side of this river?' The teacher ponders for a moment, looks up and down the river, and yells back, 'My son, you *are* on the other side.'"

Lou's guests chuckled and reflected.

"How this turned into a Zen party, I'll never know," Lou continued, acknowledging the cordial laughter. "It must have something to do with LouAnn. You may know that the Japanese characters on that banner over there stand for *ichi-go ichi-e*, the Zen concept of transience. My brilliant daughter is about to move on. In a few months, she'll become one of the first women doctoral candidates at MIT.

"But first, we travel. Tomorrow we leave for Japan on personal quests for knowledge. I am touched that you can share tonight with us. *Ichi-go ichi-e*. One time, one meeting. This moment will not be replaced."

LouAnn looked at Jordan, who tried to smile. One by one, the guests wished LouAnn luck then returned to their own lives. Lou headed inside the cottage to sleep off the effects of the marijuana.

"Just the two of us, Billy Pilgrim," LouAnn said to Jordan.

"Just the two of us," he acknowledged.

"Why don't you head over to the fire?" LouAnn suggested. She walked to the cottage and returned with blankets. She spread one next to the fire and sat on it, pulling her legs close as she rested her chin on her knees.

"I watched you walk away just then," Jordan revealed. "I didn't like it."

"I didn't know how to tell you, Jordan. The Japan trip means a lot to my father."

"Japan. MIT. Then who knows what?"

"Something like that. I'm counting on who-knows-what."

"So what now?"

"So come here."

LouAnn lay back on the blanket and opened her kimono. Jordan undressed and moved next to her. He kissed her passionately, moving his lips to her breasts.

"Perhaps you've set your sights a little too high," she teased.

Jordan took the advice. A few minutes later, LouAnn lost control for the first time in her life. Afterward, Jordan held her close.

"I miss you already, Billy Pilgrim," she said softly.

Jordan said nothing, careful to leave a tender moment alone. He was still holding LouAnn tight as dawn broke. She thought she heard his whisper in the half-light of morning.

"I miss you too," he said.

THE CONDOLENCE CALL

Youngstown Steel's condolence committee arrived at Continuum in a black Cadillac followed by a gold Cutlass coupe. Three men exited the vehicles and approached the cottage, stopping at the screen door guarded by LouAnn Epperson and Jordan Maier.

"I'm Jennings Landry," said the bland man in the corporate suit that he wore to board meetings and funerals.

"I know who you are," said LouAnn.

"Yes," Landry said matter-of-factly. "Then let me introduce our chief counsel, Landon Daumbrelle." The legal peacock had already introduced himself with flamboyant inappropriateness by wearing a raffish double-breasted glen plaid suit with a red pocket scarf.

"I know him too," LouAnn said.

"Yes." Another nervous nod to the uncomfortably obvious. "Well, then, let me introduce you to someone you probably don't know: C. J. Russo, our chief of security."

Landry acknowledged the serious-looking man, about the same age as LouAnn and Jordan, who drove Lou Epperson's prized car from the Brier Hill Works to the cottage, then limped to the front door in a black leather jacket and aviator sunglasses.

Jordan spared LouAnn the backstory: "No introductions necessary. Charley and I are acquainted."

"Whaddayaknow, the wuss," said Russo, acknowledging his boyhood neighbor. "Nothing has changed."

"Nothing except your name," Jordan shot back.

Landry sought to diffuse the tension at the screen door. "Might we come in?"

"No, I don't think so," LouAnn said.

"I must insist. It's about your father's affairs."

"You heard her. Please leave," Jordan shot back, moving between LouAnn and the corporate thugs on the other side of the screen.

Landry intervened. "Please, gentlemen, respect." Then he turned his attention back to LouAnn. "Just a moment of your time, LouAnn. Your father was a friend and a valued member of the Youngstown Steel family. I just want to express my condolences and settle affairs."

On the Youngstown Steel side of the screen door, Russo handed Daumbrelle a kit bag embroidered with the words *Simcheck & Sons Funeral Home*. The pompous attorney began an accounting:

"Your father's personal effects are inside the bag, Ms. Epperson: wallet, eyeglasses, and a key ring. We've confiscated his ID badge and removed all keys on the key ring that might operate equipment or open files, desks, lockers, offices, and doors at our plants. Mr. Russo drove your father's car here. The keys to the vehicle have been put in the bag. The keys to your cottage remain on the key chain. You may keep the bag."

Daumbrelle extended his hand, offering LouAnn the kit bag bearing the label of a funeral home. From the other side of the screen, LouAnn returned the gesture with one of her own: her middle finger.

Jordan posed the incriminating question. "I was just wondering, Mr. Daumbrelle. How did you know the remaining key on the key chain was for the Eppersons' home?"

Landry stepped in before Daumbrelle could implicate himself further: "Perhaps this will grant us entry." He held out a Tramway railroad watch, the treasured timepiece Lou Epperson carried with him to keep linear time on schedule.

Attempting to minimize personal attachment to the Tramway and the story about it that she shared with her father, LouAnn opened the screen door and accepted the watch from Lambert.

The condolence committee followed her into her father's private sanctuary, the parlor of an isolated cottage on Mosquito Lake, miles away from the roaring steel plants that the Timekeeper ran on schedule.

LouAnn clutched the Tramway tightly with one hand, tracing the metal features of the watch with the fingers of her other hand. She could feel her father on the surface; the metal had retained the oils of his hand in its patina. Her heart pulsed with the rhythm of the elegant timepiece, as it had for her father. Who would keep time now? The question brought her back to the harsh reality of the moment.

"Excuse the mess," LouAnn said in mock apology. "I wasn't expecting company at our little crime scene. I believe you know your way around."

The condolence committee entered a room that had been trashed from floor to ceiling. They retrieved cushions from the floor, placed them back on a couch, and sat down.

"It looks as if someone was looking for something, LouAnn," Daumbrelle probed.

"You think?" she mocked. "What might that be, Landon? It's okay to call you Landon, isn't it?"

"But of course"—the rake allowed—"a bit of legal advice: you might want to report the break-in to the authorities."

"And what do you suppose that would accomplish? It seems to me the pertinent questions are these: Who broke in? What were they looking for? And did they find what they were after? Wouldn't you agree, Landon?"

"Why, yes, of course," the company lawyer responded. "Who would do such a thing so soon after your father's untimely death?"

"I'm sure no one in this room has the faintest idea," LouAnn answered sarcastically. "Yet I have the unmistakable feeling that most of us in the room have been here before. Do you have that same feeling, Landon? How about you, Mr. Russo? Or should I call you Charley, too."

Jennings Landry had not anticipated that his charade of a condolence call would deteriorate into accusations. He had not considered LouAnn Epperson's disarming intelligence, her acute suspicions, or her disdain for her father's employers. Nor had he expected to encounter a reporter from *The Examiner*, a devoted friend of Lou Epperson's daughter. Somehow, Jordan Maier knew the mysterious story of Youngstown Steel's security chief, a boyhood neighbor. *The Examiner* could be managed—Youngstown Steel was adept at manipulating coverage in the local rag—but there was no telling what trouble a maverick reporter might cause. Maier hadn't been paper-trained like *The Examiner*'s other puppies. And Landry understood that the young reporter was motivated by more than writing an obituary about his friend's father.

"A story, then," Lambert proposed. "As you know, Lou and I go back quite a few years. I hired him at our plant in Shelbyville, Tenn.; then, I brought him with me to Gadsden, Alabama, where we had a steel plant and a riverboat operation on the Coosa River. Machinist, millwright, mechanic, engineer—Lou was a master at every skill in every factory: production, operations, inventory, shipping, and security. When the Sykes Corp. assigned me to Youngstown to run Youngstown Steel, I brought Lou with me again. He was a great help in turning things around. I rewarded him with a promotion to superintendent of the Brier Hill Works, the first superintendent without an engineering degree to rise to that position. I am privileged to have made that possible for Lou. It was when Lou was promoted from the labor class to the ranks of management that I met your mother, LouAnn."

With silent cynicism, LouAnn listened to Landry's tribute until she could take no more.

"What a touching story, Mr. Landry," LouAnn replied, dripping with sarcasm. "Thank you for it. My mother told me a more amusing one."

Landry seemed pleased that his story had resonated with LouAnn and, hopefully, had disarmed her. "Why, we'd love to hear it as a remembrance to both of them," he said to her.

LouAnn replied, "My mother attended one of Youngstown Steel's more charming rituals, the tea for wives at Youngstown

Country Club. Perhaps you recall them, Mr. Landry. Tea parties were held when an 'appropriate' executive was promoted into upper management. My father may not have been appropriate, but he was essential. So upon his promotion, my mother was invited for tea.

"Mother worried that she didn't fit in with the charming and cultivated ladies that are your wives. But she came, nonetheless, to the country club to honor my father.

"Your wife was there, Mr. Lambert. She said that when you were promoted to president of the company, you bought her a Cadillac so that she could appreciate Youngstown Steel's biggest customer, General Motors, whenever she drove.

"Your wife was there, too, Mr. Daumbrelle. Here's what she said to Mrs. Lambert: 'That's so romantic. Jennings must love you very much.'

"'How nice,' said my mother with her perfect Tennessee accent.

"Then it was your wife's turn, Mr. Daumbrelle. She said her husband bought her a country club membership so she could appreciate the culture of Youngstown.

"'That's so sweet,' said Mrs. Lambert. 'Landon must love you very much.'

"'How nice,' repeated my mother.

"Your wives then asked my mother what my father bought for her upon his promotion to management.

"'Lou sent me to charm school,' my mother explained.

"'Charm school. What could you possibly learn there?' your wives asked.

"'I learned how to say, "how nice," instead of "fuck you,"' my mother said.

"Pardon my sentimentality, but I love that story. Don't you, Mr. Landry?" LouAnn asked the president of Youngstown Steel.

Jennings Landry could only manage the one word that acknowledged every uncomfortable situation for him: "Yes." Learning that LouAnn was given her mother's temperament as well as her father's practicality, Landry opted for tough love. He decided to play parent and scare the crap out of two disrespectful and annoying children.

"Since things have become ugly, perhaps we should address the realities of the situation we find ourselves in," Jennings Landry began.

"First, let me disabuse you, LouAnn, of any involvement by Youngstown Steel in your father's death and the unfortunate circumstances that have occurred since. You will be held accountable for falsely accusing me or any executive in our company with a crime. Lou was my colleague and a valued member of the Youngstown Steel family. He died in an accident in the mill. We came to his aid. We shall miss him deeply. I came here today to offer my assistance and my sincere condolences, intentions which seem to have been misjudged. It is time for you to accept my sympathy, LouAnn, to get on an airplane, and head back to school before I am forced to either spank you or sue you for slander.

"Second, there are certain proprietary documents that were in your father's possession that impact this company. They are the property of Youngstown Steel and, by law, must be returned to the company. That is why Mr. Daumbrelle is here.

"Third, events will unfold tomorrow that affect the welfare of Youngstown and the nation. These events may be met with disruption. That is why Mr. Russo is here.

"I also want to caution you, Mr. Maier, about engaging in any creative writing that you might mistakenly confuse for heroic reporting. Events have been set in motion that you cannot change. Your publisher and your editors have been briefed on the role the newspaper is to play in these events. If you attempt to interfere in Youngstown Steel's affairs, Youngstown Steel will work with your employer to destroy what remains of a career that has yet to reach a small measure of mediocrity.

"So now I say to you both: behave or suffer the consequences."

If Jennings Landry had planned to intimidate two college friends reunited in a dangerous twist of time, he could not have received a more unexpected response.

"You killed my father, you son of a bitch," LouAnn said calmly. "Now get the fuck out of my house."

UNINTENDED CONSEQUENCES

The memory of the day when Jordan last saw "C. J. Russo" flashed back. He was only twelve, but he knew instinctively that survival was crucial in Youngstown. He rose early, dressing as his parents slept in the modest house on Roslyn Drive on the city's north side. Grabbing his baseball glove and a rubber ball, he walked out of the house into the backyard to play.

The yard was a perfect playground, a makeshift baseball field. Hedgerows created borders on two sides. The detached garage on the neighboring lot defined the third side of the field, creating a protected field between the hedges and the structure. Imagination filled in the rest.

Jordan set two cinder blocks at the foundation of the garage, positioned to rebound a ball thrown at the blocks from different angles. A pitch that struck the top block created a grounder that could elude the infielder for a hit or fielded for an out. A pitch that struck the lower block returned a rebound in the strike zone or slightly out—strikes and balls. A pitch striking the sharp edge of the protruding lower block would send the ball skyward into a fly ball that could be caught, sail over the fielder's head for extra bases or over the hedge for a home run. It didn't take much imagination to simulate a Major League Baseball game where the boy was the star as well as its only player.

Escapism had its interruptions. His parents or the neighbors next door might wander unexpectedly into the backyard. Constrained by a gritty and dangerous existence, they could not be expected to see the field of dreams that flowed from Jordan's imagination. They could never understand that kind of beauty in Youngstown.

So Jordan played alone, carefully choosing the time for his private escape. It was the morning of Friday, November 23, the day after Thanksgiving. Youngstown was taking the day off, sleeping in.

The north side was quiet but for the distant murmur of machinery from the mills down in the Mahoning River valley. It was a mild day for late November, perfect for the fall classic. Lead by Roger Maris, who a year earlier broke Babe Ruth's single-season home run record, the New York Yankees won their twentieth championship. In his imaginary world, the boy was mightier than Maris. Although the baseball season had ended more than a month earlier, in his mind, the boy intended to change the outcome of the 1962 World Series.

Three pitches into his fantasy series, Jordan heard muted sounds coming from the garage. He suspended his game as a man with shiny hair, slicked back from his forehead, walked from the side door of the garage. The man was wearing the bib overalls that mechanics donned over clothing. Jordan noticed that he carried tools in the large pockets.

Seeing the boy with the baseball glove and ball, the man in the overalls stopped in his tracks. His piercing eyes looked straight through the boy and into his imagination.

"Who's winning?" the man asked.

Surprised by the intrusion and the unexpected question, Jordan stood mute.

"You should play somewhere else, son," said the man in the overalls.

With that, the man turned and walked from the garage to the alley behind it. Jordan watched him follow the alley to an intersection where a two-tone DeSoto was parked. Reaching the back of the vehicle, the man slipped off the overalls and stashed them in the trunk. A second man—older, pudgy, and bald on top—emerged from the driver's side. The two embraced, entered the car, and drove off in the DeSoto.

You should play somewhere else, son.

It was a warning, a message carrying unintended consequences. *Son.*

There was that word. It was spoken with parental privilege. His father used the word *son* when logic failed to convince. *I know it seems harmless, son, but...*

Now a stranger who's not his father appeared from nowhere, warned him to move, and used the word *son.*

I'm not your son. I'll play where I want.

Ignoring the warning from the stranger, Jordan waited for the coast to clear before resuming his game.

The next disruption came a few moments later when Charles Carabbia and his two sons, Tommy and Charlie Jr., walked out of the house next door and headed toward their garage. For a moment, everyone froze.

* * *

Charles Carabbia identified himself around town as an importer of Italian wine and as an aficionado of Italian racing cars. He would have liked to been known as Ferrari Charlie, but the nickname didn't fit. He was better known around town as Cadillac Charlie for reasons that had little to do with automobiles, American, Italian, or otherwise.

The "importer" was popular with winos and fellow Italians in Youngstown whose favored drink was Gallo muscatel, a sweet fortified wine that tastes like juice from fermented raisin. Carabbia would regale *la famiglia* with stories about his trips to Italy to smuggle bottles of Gallo muscatel into the US No one seemed to mind that the Gallo winery was located in California's Sonoma Valley.

In fact, Carabbia didn't know the difference between a wine merchant and a bootlegger. He was fortunate to find a home on Youngstown's north side. If Youngstown had not been established as a haven for thugs and murderers, Carabbia would have been sent back to Italy to swig cheap wine and bet on bocce.

Immigration authorities had been trying for decades to deport Charlie to his native country, saying he entered the United States illegally as a stowaway on a ship that docked in New Orleans. He found sanctuary in Youngstown, where his nefarious activities were excused. Carabbia would be deported out of town one day, one way or the other.

Youngstown was notorious for being what was known as "wide open." It meant that illegal activities such as gambling were not only tolerated but also encouraged. "Wide open" was a community-operating plan. It guided the city's economy, law enforcement, businesses, politics, education, sports, and even its churches, which were principally funded by gaming activities run by the mob. "Open" was the deal that enabled small-time thugs like Cadillac Charlie Carabbia to assimilate seamlessly into Youngstown society.

It was in this culture that most everyone knew Cadillac Charlie's true vocation: small-time hoodlum and numbers runner. Charles Carabbia was a low-level thug associated with the Cleveland crime family that ran high-stakes dice games, the numbers rackets, and the cigarette vending machine business in Youngstown. His nickname came from his apprenticeship as a driver for a mob boss, not for his knowledge of American luxury cars. The mob bosses traveled in Cadillac Fleetwood limousines driven by cronies too dumb to be trusted with crimes requiring more than half a brain. Charlie's colleagues anointed him "Cadillac" in mock tribute to the dim-witted driver's affront to style and ability.

In Youngstown, Carabbia rose to a level of gangland mediocrity by running numbers, collecting gambling debts, and emptying vending machines. He skimmed enough money to buy the house on Roslyn Drive where he lived with his wife, Helen, and their two sons.

Youngstown was a city where a thug might live next to a judge. On respectable Roslyn Drive, the Carabbia family maintained distance and privacy from their neighbors. Even though the Carabbia boys were about the same age as the boy in the house next door, they barely acknowledged their neighbor.

* * *

"I thought I heard something out here," Cadillac Charlie said as he spotted the boy at the side of his garage.

"It's just the wuss," Charlie Jr., better known as C. J., said dismissively.

Tommy Carabbia, the runt of the litter, immediately sought to impress his bully brother. "Yeah, you wuss," he yelled at the neighbor boy. "We're going to football practice."

In his practice uniform, Tommy looked like a character from a Peanuts cartoon. The slight eleven-year-old wore an oversized sweatshirt that read "St. Edward's," football pants that hung over his knees, and droopy green socks that covered his legs. His shiny white football spikes looked as if they had never displaced a blade of grass.

"Wuss," the runt yelled again, but it came out as a pitiful squeak.

"Leave him be," Cadillac Charlie scolded his sons.

The three Carabbias walked into the garage together and piled into the car. The neighbor boy resumed his game, throwing the next pitch toward the garage just as Cadillac Charlie started his 1956 Ford Fairlane Crown Victoria.

The ball never rebounded. As it reached the cinder blocks, an explosion tore open the side of the garage with a force that lifted Jordan from the ground. Shards and planks from the wooden garage whistled past him. As if launched sideways from a rocket, he was hurtled above the ground, a human projectile flying amid the debris. When he hit the ground, every molecule of oxygen was expelled from his chest.

Jordan lay paralyzed, indifferent to pain, struggling to breathe in the dead calm that followed the chaos. His next thought was about guilt.

What have I done?

Pain overtook the attempt to understand. It rose from his core and spread to his extremities. Then came a second, more terrifying thought: *How am I going to explain this to my father?*

It was in the moments that followed that the boy prayed for the first time in his life.

God, if you make this go away, I promise never to do anything bad again.

As his prayer went unanswered, Jordan realized he was on his own. He tried to summon strength but was unable to move.

His body covered by debris, he managed to look upward where he saw a surreal scene through blurred vision: twisted metal from a Ford hanging from the electrical lines that dangled above him. Vision was followed by the slow return of his other senses. Jordan managed to move his fingers, then his hand, and then his arms. Fanning the debris around his body to get his bearings, he touched something soft and warm. Clutching it with his hand, he slowly pulled it toward his eyes. It was covered in blood and green fabric. Then he saw the white spikes attached to the limb. He was holding Tommy Carabbia's disembodied leg.

The realization brought a scream so deep and so primal that Jordan didn't recognize it as his own. It consumed him as he slipped into a deep state of unconsciousness, silent but for the distant murmur of the steel mills.

PART TWO

TWIST OF THE WIND

ANTITRUST

Three days earlier

Jennings Landry had been preparing his entire career for this meeting. Create a scandalous strategy benefitting the interests of a few powerful industrial barons, and justify it as a rational business case serving the national economy. He would only have to convince the attorney general of the United States.

There was a certain symmetry about the meeting in a government office halfway between the White House and the Capitol on Pennsylvania Avenue. The man who occupied the office had been Landry's law professor at Tulane. With his methodical Southern manner and blunt assessment of Landry's potential in interpreting the law, Winston Dell III advised an otherwise promising student to find a profession more worthy of deceit: corporate management.

Landry well understood his limitations, as well as his potential. With a slight shift in the wind, he transferred to Tulane's business school to master the art of corporate chicanery under the tutelage of the slick, golden-tongue judge who cut a smooth Cajun two-step with society courtesans, overmatched legal weasels, and gentlemen-crooks who ran Louisiana like rapacious kings descended from France.

WD3, as he was known, not only blessed Landry's transfer to Tulane's clubby business school, he advocated it. The transfer was engineered by New Orleans shipping and steel profiteer Schuyler Sykes. A generous donor to Tulane's A. B. Freeman School of Business,

Sykes underwrote Landry's education, paying WD3 handsomely to nurture the prodigy's potential for a career in pelf and deceit.

Hired by Sykes upon his graduation from Tulane, Landry rose to meet the expectations of his mentor. He quickly exhibited the distinctive New Orleans knack for genteel arrogance and social order amid the messy Louisiana gumbo of corrupt politicians, reckless business manipulators, displaced mobsters, oil refiners, Cajun rednecks, and bayou shippers. Landry had the business voodoo, the magic pin doll for cleaning up a mess. And Schuyler Sykes had a mess.

Since he acquired a grimy steel company up north, Sykes' fortunes became murkier than the Mississippi. With his family's shipping business sinking, Sykes raided the coffers of the steel mills he had acquired. Steelmaking was the lynchpin of the American economy, a capital-intensive industry that belched money. Sykes skimmed the profits of his steel mills, failing to reinvest in outdated properties requiring continual modernization. Committed only to Sykes Brothers Steamship Lines, the business founded by his father to move cargo up the Mississippi and later, during the Vietnam War, into the Mekong Delta, Schuyler schemed to drain the cesspool. He sent Jennings Landry to Ohio to run Youngstown Steel into the ground, find a buyer, and get out of town with his pockets full.

Landry liked the steel industry even less than Sykes, but he knew how to maximize profits: Cut costs. Create efficiencies. Minimize capital investment. Solve the problem. Do what's necessary.

Landry followed the script, first at Sykes's small steel plant in Shelbyville, Tennessee, then at the big plant in Gadsden, Alabama, an hour northeast of Birmingham. It was surprisingly easy to increase production and profits with fewer non-union millwrights willing to work for less pay just to have a job. Landry was rewarded with the job he loathed in a place he despised: president of Youngstown Steel in godforsaken Youngstown and Pittsburgh without the charm. His current move: find a way to return to New Orleans with his pockets full and his reputation intact.

On September 12, 1977, Landry came to a more suitable setting for his skills, at least in his mind: the office of the attorney general of the United States. Inspired by the aura of Washington, Lambert couldn't help but wonder, *Pull this off and who knows? Return to New Orleans. Run for Congress. Must make an impression on WD3.* Jennings Landry was ready, even for Winston Dell III.

* * *

"I see you took my advice," WD3 said to his former student as they entered the private conference room of the attorney general. "Come meet some real lawyers."

The attorney general's team was already seated around the mahogany conference table: a bookish clerk hauling a portfolio of files, a patrician-looking white man in a Brooks Brothers suit, and a stout black woman who was setting up her portable stenotype machine. Shaking hands with no one and ignoring the visiting counsel for Youngstown Steel, WD3 sat down at the conference table and turned to the woman with the stenotype.

"We should get the preliminaries down for the record, Miz Felecia," WD3 announced firmly yet ever so politely. Then he turned to face the men around the table. "Miz Felecia Rucker-Rogers here is gonna type into that machine of hers and keep a record of our little conversation. She knows how to tidy things up. I assume there are no objections?

"Well, then, let's proceed. I am Winston Dell III, attor*neee* general of these United States. I am joined by Mr. John Steverson, assistant attorney general for the Justice Department's Antitrust Division, and by Mr. Lionel Koda, principal investigator. We are here to discuss the preliminary finding of the staff on the matter of the proposed merger between Youngstown Steel of Youngstown, Ohio, and the Jones & Laughlin Steel Company of Pittsburgh, Pennsylvania.

WD3 caught himself then pivoted. "Where are my manners?" he said. "I have yet to make proper introductions. We are joined by the estimable Jennings Landry, the president and chief executive of Youngstown Steel.

"I should tell you boys that Mr. Koda has led the investigation and written the report we're 'bout to consider—sorta playbook on mergers and competition. Lots of fine facts and good words. Int'restin' story, too. I trust you have read it."

Landon Daumbrelle walked into the ambush before Jennings Landry could stop him.

"There's more to that story, Mr. Attorney Gen—"

WD3 cut him off at the mouth. "Have we been properly introduced, sir?"

Daumbrelle could only manage "Er, well, not exactly."

"You may address me as Judge Dell, son, in deference to my long service on the federal bench. Now, who might you be?"

"Landon Daumbrelle, chief counsel and vice president of Youngstown Steel—"

"Of course you are," WD3 interrupted. "Mr. Dumb-*bell*, did you say? That's a right unfortunate name for a lawyer."

"Daum-*brelle*. It's French-Creole."

"I'm sure it is." WD3 turned to his stenographer. "Miz Felecia, would you be sure to get *Mr. Daumbrelle's* name spelled with all the letters in the right places. We wouldn't want to encourage an unfortunate pronunciation in the record."

WD3 opened the large file before him on the conference table, silently sorted the papers on the top of the file, leaned back in his chair, and closed his eyes.

"Judge Bell, if I may…" Jennings Landry began.

"Is that you, Jennings?" WD3 answered, his eyes still closed. "Still trying to play lawyer? Don't wet that fancy suit of yours just yet."

Those in the room waited for WD3 to open his eyes and wondered what he would say next.

"You know, Jennings, these antee-trust cases aren't 'zactly my cup of Southern comfort. I'm just a simple civil rights lawyer from Georgia who lawyered hisself up to the federal bench, got to know the gov'ner, had no idea he'd become president and have the good sense to make me attorney general. Int'restin' job. Confusin' too. Washington sure ain't Nawlins.

"That's why I got me some Harvard lawyers when I came to the swamp. My apologies, John, I've neglected to introduce you to the Louisiana clan of Youngstown Steel. This here is John Steverson, assistant attorney general of the Antitrust Division of the Department of Justice for these United States. John here is the smartest sumbitch to ever look at fancy deals between conspiring corporate crooks."

Shot down before they started, Landry and Daumbrelle bit their tongues. *Say nothing until the judge gives you permission.*

WD3 picked up Koda's report on the conference table. "I've been thinking on this," WD3 said. "The thing is, Jennings, this dog won't hunt. Mr. Koda and Mr. Steverson say your little merger might eliminate competition in the steel industry. It would raise prices on just about everything we build in this county. Hurt a lot of good people too. Cost them their jobs. Jobs is damn hard to get these days. Real costly to buy a home in this economy too. What are those mortgage rates, Lionel—10, 12 percent? Can't even find gas for all those Jap cars. This mess in the Ay-rab countries goin' get worse too."

Landry and Daumbrelle held their breath.

"Tell the truth, I don't like telling companies what to do," WD3 continued. "I may not like what they do, but they have a right to do it. Make a few bucks, good for the economy. That's the American way. Don't like it tal,' but there it is. Mr. Steverson, he's the smart one on these antee-trust cases. He and I have been lawyering on it. You got something to say now, Jennings? It's your turn to talk."

The student took a page from the master: disarm, charm, then strike.

"Yes, sir. I was going to ask Mr. Daumbrelle to make the legal case, but as you've observed so astutely, my son-in-law has a problem with protocol. I can't say I approved of him marrying my daughter. But what's a proper *New Awlins* family to do?" Landry asked, emphasizing the pronunciation that distinguishes proper New Orleans denizens from word-dragging Southerners and voodoo rednecks trying to impress.

Landry detected a smile of approval from WD3, who understood the distinction.

"So, Mr. Attorney General, let me make the case straight ahead. It's a business case, not a legal one. We're happy to let the legal boys sort out the whereases and what-fors. What I want to talk to you about is steel—the nation's industry. We're about to lose that industry and maybe our cars, ships, and oil too. And if we do, we can just turn our economy over to the Japs and Arabs."

WD3 may have served his own mythology in a colorful career, but he was an uncompromising ally of Jimmy Carter, a president trying to fix a struggling American economy and defining a place for the United States in a tense, increasingly unfamiliar and unforgiving world.

"I'm listening, Jennings. You now have the attention of the attorney general of these United States. But I caution you, Jennings. No lagniappe. You and I know what that word means. I won't have it. Embellish the facts, and I'll cut off your cojones and celebrate by grinnin' like a possum eatin' a sweet potato."

"Thank you, Judge. I'd just assume keep mine."

Jennings Landry had learned. In the minutes that followed, he made a compelling case for a US policy that would finance the modernization of industrial America and shut down costly, aging plants. The policy would enable mergers and acquisitions otherwise prohibited by antitrust law, mergers such as the one between Youngstown Steel and Jones & Laughlin Steel that the Antitrust Division was investigating.

WD3 was impressed by his former student's argument, but also troubled by it. He grasped the situation immediately, a trait that propelled him from New Orleans power brokering to the federal bench to the attorney general's office.

He considered the implications for the Carter administration in a world that was flashing out of control. Deny the merger, and light a fire of plant closings throughout the steel industry—5,000 jobs to start, then tens of thousands more as the dominos fell. In that scenario, the president loses the support of labor for eliminating jobs and might well lose the backbone of the US economy—manufacturing. Approve the merger and save jobs—except those in Youngstown. Approval would be unpopular there, but the Carter administration had three years to contain the Youngstown problem and stave off the Japanese before the next election three years off.

The lead investigator for the Justice Department's Antitrust Division wasn't having any of it.

"Antitrust laws explicitly prevent mergers and acquisitions that reduce competition, particularly if they were conceived merely to improve the balance sheet of one of the players," Lionel Koda argued. "The burden of proof here is on Youngstown Steel. Our investigation raises questions whether the company is really failing or whether it is simply mismanaged."

WD3 turned the case back to Landry. "That's quite a question Mr. Koda has raised. Don't you think, Jennings?"

Landry shook his head.

"Before you go defending your management capabilities—capabilities of which I am personally acquainted—I want to make you aware of another problem, Jennings. We have received evidence that things aren't as bleak as you would have us believe."

"What kind of evidence?" Landry asked.

"I reckon that would be telling," WD3 replied. "I can only tell you that Mr. Koda and Mr. Steverson find it strangely compelling. It seems you have a whistleblower in your ranks."

"That, sir, is highly unlikely," Landry replied. "Our ranks are closed. We have taken care to make our case for the merger with extensive data, exhaustive analysis, and proprietary records known only to the management team."

"And yet there is this, ah, evidence, Jennings. You can't put wishes in one hand and manure in the other and see which one fills up first. What do you think, John?"

"The law gives broad discretion to the government to either sanction or oppose a merger such as the one proposed by Youngtown Steel," Steverson explained. "To meet the antitrust standard for a merger in one of nation's most critical sectors, the preponderance of evidence must be overwhelming."

"Put that in words acoupla *Nawlins* boys would understand. Will you, John?"

Steverson responded succinctly to the attorney general. "The case must be clean."

"There it is," WD3 said. "Like I said, Jennings, this dog won't hunt. Tidy things up, and we might get to talk again."

LEVERAGE

Winston Dell III worried that he had overplayed the charming Southern lawyer routine at the meeting with Youngstown's Steel execs. His top lieutenants in Justice's Antitrust Division had witnessed this kind of performance before. It was a signal that the attorney general was conflicted.

Nine months in office, the attorney general was at his most disarming when he was vulnerable. The postmeeting debriefing with Youngstown Steel's executives was intended to eliminate any vulnerability in a complex case in which WD3 was personally associated.

"I've known Jennings Lambert since he was suckin' on his momma's teets," WD3 admitted. "I tutored him for Schuyler Sykes, a scoundrel of the first order but probably not the biggest crook to run money up the Mississippi."

"That could be a problem for us, Mr. Attorney General," warned Lionel Koda, the Antitrust Division's circumspect chief investigator,

"Are you suggesting a conflict of interest, Lionel?" WD3 asked, warning Koda. "I've never had a conversation with the Sykes clan that didn't make we want to change my clothes. But they ain't stupid. Lot of powerful corporate hacks on Youngstown Steel's side. What do you think, John?"

It was John Steverson's job to dismiss any doubts about the attorney general's authority or credibility.

"You were a federal judge, legal scholar, and law professor in New Orleans," Steverson pointed out. "Then a preeminent attorney in Georgia and Washington who wrote the Civil Rights Act. That experience makes you informed and experienced, not compromised. President Carter knew what he was doing when he put you in this office."

"Mebbe," the attorney general said.

WD3 had moved on. He was already deep into his undeniable talent: formulating a metaphor which reduced complex legal cases to their essence.

"You ever been to Mother's on Poydras Street in New Orleans, John?" he asked his Antitrust chief. "They shred and simmer roast beef, leaving the drippings at the bottom of the pan. They call the falling-apart meat 'debris.' Then they stack the debris on a crusty bun so that it only soaks the bottom part of the bread. You can dress it with cabbage, a pickle, mayo, and mustard, but you're still feasting on the juices and dregs of overcooked beef. Debris. Folks line up outside the door to get themselves a debris samwich from Mother's.

"This case is like that, boys. It's falling apart, but you gotta appreciate the pan drippings. Who'd have thought that Jennings Landry and his falling-apart steel company could mess with so many jobs and America's economic policies? Yep. What we've got here is a debris samwich."

Steverson thoroughly understood WD3's colorful culinary metaphor. He wasn't about to discount his boss or, for that matter, Jennings Landry and his proposed merger.

"Landry has made a compelling case," he explained. "Outside of a few thousand steelworkers in Youngstown, he has support with influential interests. The merger case is solid. It may even prove popular, even though Lionel's staff report raises doubts. We can't be seen as interfering with business decisions of public companies. But we've got cover no matter what we choose to do."

"Cover?" Lionel Koda protested. "The merger is anticompetitive, John. A lot of people in Youngstown are going to those their jobs because New Orleans overseers ran the steel mills—the city's economic lynchpin—into the ground."

WD3 got the point. "Okay, Lionel. Then please tell me that we have something more to prevent the president from sanctioning massive job losses that light a fuse that puts the nation's economy at risk."

"Video tapes," Koda disclosed. "Lots of video tapes purporting to show images of giant swings in inventory at Youngstown Steel."

"And that means what?" WD3 asked.

The head of the Antitrust Division stepped in to answer. "A viable business. Sufficient business activity would refute Youngstown Steel's contention that it is a failing company," Steverson explained. "That would undermine the case for a merger."

"Well, well, isn't that a pot of spicy gumbo." WD3 huffed. "I think you were saying somethin' about video tapes. Weren't you, Lionel?"

"Yes, sir. An anonymous whistleblower supplied us with dozens of tapes," Koda explained.

"How damaging is the evidence from the whistleblower?" Steverson asked.

"At the moment, not damaging at all," Koda replied. "The tapes are more mystery than evidence."

WD3 was growing impatient with Koda. "I brought up the whistleblower scenario to spook Jennings," he scolded his investigator. "So I hope you're not going to tell me we don't have anythin' to take that sumbitch down."

"Well, actually, we can't watch the tapes," Koda admitted.

"And we can't watch them because?" asked WD3.

"We don't have a way to play them," Koda explained. "You're not going to like this next part. The tapes were made on a Japanese video camera, advanced technology superior to our own. To play them, we apparently require a video cassette player, a prototype manufactured in Japan that's compatible with the camera."

"Please tell me that you're messin' with me, Lionel," WD3 told his investigator.

"I'm afraid not, sir."

"Well, let's see if we can get us some of them—what did you call them? Video cassette players? To watch those tapes and see if we can discredit an attempt to manipulate government policy," WD3 suggested.

Steverson saw the advanced version of the problem.

"I'm afraid that puts in a difficult situation, Mr. Attorney General," the chief of the Antitrust Division explained. "First, we'd have to acknowledge to the Japanese that we need their equipment to solve a problem we have in setting US trade policy. Yes, they would know. The Japanese, our trade enemy, would then use this information to demonstrate their superiority in technology. An additional irony would come to public light: a US steel company used Japanese technology to demonstrate that our steel industry was, in fact, inferior to theirs—which, of course, is at the core of our policy decision. Such disclosures could impact markets for steel and automobiles in the US, Japan, and the world. President Carter couldn't survive the economic turmoil, particularly in light of the escalating oil crisis. He would not be reelected."

As usual, WD3 found a way out.

"Now that's a fine mess that we obviously can't have. Let's make it Jennings's problem," WD3 schemed. "That scoundrel knows we have something, but he doesn't know what. That makes him paranoid and desperate, his own worst enemy. We play like we've got the goods on him, never divulging that we have video tapes that we can't even watch. Let Jennings deal with his debris. I'll deal with the president. That'll be all, gentlemen."

BOILERMAKERS

Jennings Landry wanted to feel good about the meeting with Winston Dell III. He had made a compelling argument—precise, informed, meaningful, and persuasive—to the attorney general of the United States. He stated his case with confidence and charm. He even managed to captivate his former teacher and foil the irrepressible WD3. Yet he left the meeting depressed and uncertain.

"I think we won, boss," Landon Daumbrelle declared, trying to cheer up the concerned Youngstown Steel president. "Let's celebrate with a drink."

Landry wasn't ready to declare victory, let alone drink with Landon. He had quite enough of the clueless Sykes family scion placed under his wing and into his family. Jennings answered like a discouraged father-in-law dismissing the ne'er-do-well who married his daughter: "Not now, Landon," he replied. "I think I'll walk a bit. Alone. Meet me in an hour at the rooftop bar of the hotel."

It was only five blocks from the Justice Department to the Hotel Washington. Landry relished the walk along Pennsylvania Avenue to the White House, then the short jog north along Pershing Park to the hotel. The slow walk took less than ten minutes, but Landry needed a full hour to calm himself for another meeting with his clueless son-in-law.

The open-air bar of the Hotel Washington afforded the capitol's best view of the powerful. Put in his place by the attorney general, Landry fulfilled a need to be in the presence of a higher power. At the rooftop bar eleven stories up, he claimed a perch overlooking the address across the street: 1600 Pennsylvania Avenue. There he ordered his first martini.

Daumbrelle arrived early and ordered a Dewar's on the rocks. "So that's the White House," the New Orleans dandy observed. "Not exactly Garden District material."

Landry was sipping on his second martini with enthusiasm. He ignored Landon's attempt at hometown humor, changing the subject. "Landon, I'm sorry I embarrassed you at the meeting. I was just trying to reestablish a connection with Winston. I should not have done so at your expense."

"Goes with the title," Youngstown Steel's vice president said.

"I'd like to talk with you about that," Landry said gently. "It was your responsibility to contain our little plan, was it not? Where did things go wrong?"

Landon didn't have a clue.

"The *evidence*," Landry explained. "You do recall the attorney general mentioning the unfortunate evidence that had been brought to the attention of the Antitrust Division?"

"Not exactly."

"This dog won't hunt?" Landry mimicked WD3 in a dead-on impression.

"That was a shame about his dog."

"Dear god, you thought he was talking about his dog?"

"Well…I like dogs."

"Do you know the meaning of the word *whistleblower*?" Landry asked. "It's—"

"I know what it means."

"Good. Has it occurred to you that we have a whistleblower in our ranks who is trying to scuttle the merger with information that damages our case?"

"So someone is whistling?" Daumbrelle asked painfully.

"Landon, I want you to listen carefully. Think. Who knows about our plans to close the Campbell Works?"

"There's the executive team: that would be you and me."

"Yes. And?"

"Ray Wozniak, the Campbell Works superintendent."

"Yes, Wozniak. He has been blessed. Do you know your Bible, Landon? 'Behold, I send you forth as sheep in the middle of wolves: be you therefore wise as serpents, and harmless as doves.'"

"Matthew 10:16. The lawyer's verse."

"Quite right. The shepherd Wozniak has been sent forth as a sheep. The poor man has been relocated to Tampa where's he's medicating his memory loss with rum and Coke, spending his retirement days betting on jai alai games. Harmless as a dove. So that leaves whom?"

"Maybe Lou Epperson," Landon said weakly.

"Maybe Lou Epperson?"

"I guess so. He receives operational reports and supervises Brier Hill."

"Now you're making sense."

"Lou's doing the whistling?"

"Who else? We must get to him. If we can't stop him from proving that the Youngstown mills are profitable despite our best efforts to manage them into oblivion, then the Justice Department will have to rule that the failing company exception to antitrust law does not apply. In other words, we lose. That is not a scenario we can tolerate. Cousin Schuyler and the family will sentence us to live out our remaining days in Youngstown removing turds from the Mahoning River."

"I see."

"No, you don't see. Listen to me carefully. I want you to take care of the Epperson problem. Lou's a Boy Scout. He's got a merit badge for every part of the mill. That's the bad part: he knows everything. The other bad part: he's management, but the workers treat him like their brother. What he says matters."

"I understand."

"I don't think you do. Epperson must be silenced and discredited. I want you to deal with this."

"I'll call Russo. We'll handle it."

"Good man. One more thing. I can't be implicated in any way. The attorney general and I go way back together. He knows me. Understand? Say it again: Jennings can't be implicated in any way."

"Jennings can't be implicated in any way."

"Good. Now, let's have a real drink." Landry hailed a bar babe wearing a vest, flared pants, and platform heels. He asked her to bring four boilermakers.

"I'm afraid I don't know that drink," the bar babe admitted.

"A shot and a beer. Two for each of us."

The server was still puzzled.

"Bring four mugs of beer—Budweiser or Schlitz, nothing imported. Four shots of whiskey too. Jack Daniels would be fine."

The bar babe obliged. She returned with the mugs of beer and shots of whiskey, placing them in two rows on the table. "Your boilermakers, gentlemen."

"Here's how they do it in steel country." Landry demonstrated. He emptied one shot into a mug of beer. Then he lifted the mug and downed the entire drink with one long draw, not lifting his lips from the mug until all the beer and whiskey were consumed.

"Full Youngstown," he said, finishing the drink, suds hanging on his upper lip. "Now, for the executive version."

Landry asked the bar babe if she had heard of a depth charge. "Let me demonstrate." He dropped another whiskey-filled shot glass into the bottom of the second beer-filled mug. Again, he sucked down the contents in one long draw, but this time, finishing with the empty shot glass between his lips. Removing the shot glass from his mouth, he returned the two empty vessels to the table.

"A true leader must acquire talents that are unexpected yet necessary," he proclaimed. Then he belched loudly.

By now, the drinking exhibition had caught the attention of the regular crowd at Point of View or POV, as the rooftop bar was known. Landry stood with his third boilermaker and addressed the astonished group whose whispered lobbying had been disturbed. Sufficiently lubricated from the pain of the day, Lambert rose to ask for understanding.

"Good citizens of Washington, D.C., I stand humbly before you to beg your indulgence. I am a guest in my nation's capitol, and I have behaved crudely against my better intentions. The urgency of my ambitions and the excitement of the day have caused me to forget my usual good manners and Southern decorum. You have my sincere apolo—"

Landry belched again, deep and long, before he could get the last word out.

After acknowledging the applause from the patrons, Jennings Landry downed his third boilermaker. Then the tipsy Youngstown Steel president managed to stumble down to the lobby, check out of the hotel, catch a cab to nearby National Airport, and board a prop plane for the short bumpy flight back to Youngstown. Drunk and defeated, he considered how to deal with The Timekeeper as he heaved repeatedly into an airsickness bag.

DEATH OF THE TIMEKEEPER

Emboldened by the confrontation at the cottage, Jordan Maier demanded to cover Youngstown Steel's press conference announcing its closing of the Campbell Works. Jordan was onto something, but *The Examiner*'s editors didn't trust the unpredictable reporter who had ambitions beyond his current assignment of writing obituaries. Further, he resisted *The Examiner Way*, the newspaper's stylebook for bland, no-drama, stay-out-of-trouble, get-along/go-along reporting.

There was an additional concern: Jennings Landry. Placing a call to the newspaper's publisher, Landry attempted to disqualify Maier from handling any story that touched Youngstown Steel. He characterized Maier as a misguided young reporter with a vivid imagination and a creative interpretation of facts. Landry insisted that coverage of his company's news event would be better handled by the compliant eunuch known as Weezer—George Wease, the newspaper's business reporter.

Learning that Wease would likely be assigned to cover the press conference, Jordan dared to question *The Examiner*'s mission.

"So the idea is to have Weezer help Jennings Landry screw over the city," he protested loudly. "When exactly did we lose our balls?"

The insubordinate question rose above the din of the newsroom, hanging in the air for all *The Examiner* eunuchs to hear. They gasped in unison at the sexist, anatomically flawed metaphor hurled in the general direction of Youngstown's guardian angel, Managing Editor Annie Przybylski.

Przybylski responded with calm and firmness. "Fortunately for you, I was born without a penis or testicles," she said. "If I had them, you'd be gone."

Unapologetic, Jordan wasn't about to be pushed out of *his* story, let alone turn it over to Weezer—a wheezing hack masquerading as a reporter. Besides, solving the mystery of Lou Epperson's death became a personal quest the moment LouAnn uttered those words: *Billy Pilgrim, is that you? Where have you been?*

As Przybylski huddled with her editors, Jordan awaited reprimand, suspension, or firing. He had stopped worrying about it. He was on a mission to uncover Youngstown Steel's motives, expose Jennings Landry's criminal manipulations, and solve Lou Epperson's murder, whether or not he worked for the hometown rag.

Maier had not, however, anticipated the degree to which Przybylski and the typically accommodating editors of *The Examiner* were offended by the shameless attempt by Landry to manipulate coverage. The editors agreed to placate the publisher by sending Weezer to Youngstown Steel headquarters to cover the Youngstown Steel press conference. But they also acted on an idea that had long been suppressed at *The Examiner*: journalism matters in times of crisis.

Disciplinary action could wait. Maier was instructed to finish the obituary that was called in by the night embalmer at Simcheck & Sons Funeral Home. He was also dispatched to the Campbell Works to cover reaction at the steel mill that was being shut down. Two hours later, he dictated just one story from a phone booth outside the gate:

> CAMPBELL—Minutes after losing their live-
> lihoods, steelworkers at Youngstown Steel's
> Campbell Works began a mournful march from
> their smoke-stained factory along the Mahoning
> River to the worker's bridge at the Poland Avenue
> gate. Each wore a company-issued hard hat with
> a strip of duct tape—a mourning band—placed

over the company logo. One by one, they crossed the bridge, uttered the name "Lou," and tossed their hard hats into the murky Mahoning. Illuminated by the morning sun, the yellow hard hats bobbed in the dead river like floating memorial candles sent out to sea.

Lou Epperson died a steelworker's death. His body was found at the bottom of an empty soaking pit, a sunken hot tub for smoldering ingots. He died with his steel-toed work boots on, hard hat next to his body. Epperson supervised the mill in which he was found dead. A spokesman for Youngstown Steel said he died in an industrial accident.

Known throughout the Steel Valley as the Timekeeper, Epperson was a steel master who guided men safely, time after time, through dangerous work and the volatile chemistry of steelmaking.

Killed in an industrial accident in his own plant? Lou?

Improbable. But today, Youngstown's steelworkers confront the improbable with the reality of the day. The Timekeeper is gone. So, too, are their jobs.

The news came without warning. Minutes after Youngstown Steel announced the closing of the Campbell Works at its corporate headquarters across town, word moved through the mill like red-hot rods shooting across casters.

Steelworkers described the scene inside mill as disorienting. According to those inside the plant, workers shut down their machines as news of the plant's imminent closing traveled from one department to the next. Steelmaking operations ceased at about 9 a.m., just two hours into the day shift. Leaving their stations, stunned steelworkers gathered in locker rooms and quiet corners of the vast factory. Some advocated damaging the equipment. Others suggested occupying the plant.

Shop stewards proposed a response that would unite rather than divide them: they could make a more powerful statement by marching silently from the plant in tribute to a fallen brother. Youngstown Steel could dismiss their workers, but they couldn't dismiss questions about one of their own. The Timekeeper would become the unifying symbol of a worker's movement for justice.

Steelworkers said that foremen and supervisors, who represent Youngstown Steel management, ordered the men back to work, but did so without conviction. They, too, had just lost their jobs. The managers remained in the tomb as the workers filed out the factory marching, one by one, in a funeral procession across the river. It took an hour for all to cross.

The scene on the other side of the bridge was surreal, evoking the feel of a cemetery after a burial, mourners consoling each other in grief and disbelief.

Vince Szabo, a stove tender in the blast furnace, was among the first to cross the bridge. He was met by a television reporter who asked him how he felt.

"How do I feel? How I'm supposed to feel," Szabo shot back. "One minute you have a job, a paycheck, a life. The next minute someone takes all of it from you. How would you feel?"

The union that represents the steelworkers at the Campbell Work was not given prior notice of the plant's closing, according to Mike Bowers, president of United Steelworkers of America Local 2332. Typically, unions are notified in advance of plant closings and major layoffs.

"This is more than an unwarranted demonstration of control," Bowers told *The Examiner*. "This is an act of cruelty that strips away the dignity of our community."

Stripped of that dignity, many of those who crossed the river seemed lost, uncertain where to go next. Some clustered around Rev. Raymond Stanczak, the pastor at Christ the Good Shepherd parish in Campbell, who had come to console steelworkers, many of whom were his parishioners.

Others wandered down Poland Avenue to open The Tap, the neighborhood tavern named for the valve that delivers draught beer as well as for the operation that taps the blast furnace for molten steel.

A third group headed to the union hall to vent their anger. Others headed home to be with their families. One was Stefan Pejic, a millwright who's worked at the Campbell Works for 40 years.

"When we were kids, we thought the steel mill was it," said Pejic, who emigrated from Croatia in 1935 to find work in Youngstown's mills. "We'd see the men comin' out, all dirty, black. The only thing white was the goggles over their eyes. We thought they were it, strong men. We just couldn't wait to get in there."

Pejic then chuckled. "It wasn't what it was cut out to be."

Pejic is now worried about just getting by. He worries about his family and four sons, all who followed their father's footsteps. "'If you ever wind up in that steel mill like me, I'm gonna hit you in the head,' is what I told them. Go get yourself a schooling. Stay out of the mills, or you'll wind up the way I did. Forty years of hard work, and what do I have to show for it? Nothing."

Then Pejic said he was going home.

Remember this date: September 19, 1977, Black Monday, the day time ran out on Youngstown.

Steelmaking is life here. Through cycles of strikes and layoffs, good times and bad, steelworkers pass their craft from one generation to the next. That ends today.

It was that realization that brought the final generation of Youngstown's steelworkers to the gate of the Campbell Works this morning. Crossing the bridge, they tossed their hard hats into a dead river then walked away from a dead steel mill in their steel-toed work boots.

On one side of the bridge, a legacy. On the other side, nothing.

"Nothing will become of nothing." Black Monday is scripted in King Lear. But this Shakespearean tragedy is also an obituary. This newspaper requires a dispassionate send-off in a simple style that treats all lives equally, with respect. Accordingly, Lou Epperson deserves a proper *Examiner* obituary:

Lou Epperson, 58, of Cortland, died Friday in an industrial accident at the Brier Hill Works of Youngstown Steel, the steel mill he supervised.

Mr. Epperson came to Youngstown 23 years ago from the steel mills of Gadsden, Alabama, to work as a foreman at the Brier Hill Works, first at the blast furnace known as "Jenny" and subsequently in mills throughout the plant. An industrial engineer without a degree, he built a reputation for managing operations and improving efficiency at every operation.

The precision by which he managed men and machines earned him the nickname "the Timekeeper." He trained hundreds of steelworkers, stressing safety in the plant's dangerous jobs. Credited with saving an aging steel plant, Mr. Epperson was named supervisor of the Brier Hills Works five years ago.

Spiritual and wise, Mr. Epperson was revered by his family. He married his high school sweetheart, Ann Ford, a teacher. They had a child, LouAnn, to whom both father and mother gave their name and devotion. Ann Ford Epperson died of breast cancer in 1972. LouAnn Epperson, a teacher at the California Institute of Technology, lives the legacy of her parents in Pasadena, CA.

A memorial service will be held at 7 p.m. this evening at United Steelworkers of America Local 2332.

There it is, a proper obituary. Dispassionate. Simple. Ordinary.

Lou Epperson was none of those things.

* * *

"That's it," Jordan Maier said to the editor taking dictation from the reporter in a phone booth outside the Campbell Works.

There was no response.

"Is it okay?" Jordan asked.

Still no response.

Jordan sensed the problem: "You're not going to run it. Are you, Annie?"

AnniePrzybylski had never considered a story quite like this one. She didn't know how to feel about it or how to answer the question from the insolent brat who embarrassed her earlier in the newsroom.

Annie was not given to taking insults personally, especially from an inexperienced rookie reporter such as Maier. In a city powered by testosterone, she had endured every conceivable put-down by sexist little men. Annie mastered self-control, affirmed by the knowledge that, given time, a patient journalist could get even with any son of a bitch.

But time was running out. The immutable deadlines that framed the daily miracle awaited a decision from the managing editor.

Hemming and hawing were not part of Annie's disposition. She prided herself on decisiveness; she apologized for nothing. A woman in a man's profession in a macho town, she outsmarted and outmaneuvered her way past the crooked politicians, corrupt cops, controlling mobsters, and duplicitous steel lords who ran Youngstown. Rising through the ranks of the boy's club known as journalism, she acquired advanced survival skills. She informed the boys that, in Polish, *Przybylski* means *he who has arrived*. And now, the only woman managing editor of a major US newspaper arrived at a decision that could break the rules—the rules that she made.

"You're not going to run it. Are you, Annie?"

The question demanded an immediate answer, not so much for the reporter who asked it, but for the editor confronting the biggest story imaginable. Maier's story would upset the balance of things in Youngstown, raising questions that civic leaders—including the publisher—would rather not consider. The implications of the story touched every aspect of life in Youngstown.

Annie wasn't sure she could trust anyone but herself with this story.

I am Youngstown's guardian angel. She *who has arrived.*

People with ordinary jobs had time to work through the implications of consequential decisions. Annie Przybylski had one minute.

"You're not going to run it. Are you, Annie?"

On deadline, Youngstown's guardian angel responded with words used by managing editors everywhere: "Let me worry about that."

Annie removed her ear set and hung up the phone before her smart-ass reporter could deliver his next insult.

Forty-five minutes later, *The Examiner* rolled off the presses with two stories on its front page. One was George Wease's apologetic coverage of Youngstown Steel closing the Campbell Works. The other was a story by Jordan Maier that ran under the headline "Death of the Timekeeper." The headline was written by Annie Przybylski.

Not a word of the story dictated from the Campbell Works had been changed. All of Youngstown read it and wept.

FLIGHT OF THE PAPER AIRPLANE

Minutes after the afternoon edition of *The Youngstown Examiner* arrived at Youngstown Steel's headquarters, Landon Daumbrelle and C. J. Russo were summoned to Jennings Landry's office. All eyes in the building turned from a story on *The Examiner*'s front page to the two execs making their way through the headquarters building to the president's office.

"Go right in. He's waiting on you," a secretary said with a boy-are-you-in-trouble tone and the look of a guidance counselor preparing two misbehaving students for a meeting with the principal.

Landry sat behind a large desk in a modern, light-filled office overlooking the park that surrounded the suburban Boardman headquarters.

Daumbrelle and Russo sat down in the two chairs across the desk from Landry, who did not look up. Instead, he fixated on the newspaper on his desk. Then he reached into a drawer, pulling out a steel ruler.

"The thing about a newspaper is that after you read it, you don't know what to do with it," Landry explained, concentrating on the newspaper under his eyes. Using the ruler as a straight edge, he tore the front page from the spine of the edition. Using the ruler again, he tore the front page in half, separating the two stories on the front page—George Wease's coverage of Youngstown Steel's press conference and a story headlined "Death of the Timekeeper" by Jordan Maier.

"You can wrap the trash with it," he continued, folding the part of the page with Maier's story. "But that can be messy. You'll end up with ink on your hands from the newsprint."

Landry continued to fold the half page. "Or you can use it as tinder to start a fire. But we don't want to start fires, do we?"

With additional folds, Landry created a triangle with wings tapering from a sharp tip to a wider bottom. "As a child, I learned a more productive use for the newspaper, one that requires ability and purpose."

He picked up the paper airplane that he had made and flicked it like a dart toward Russo. The short flight ended by crashing, point-first, into Russo's forehead.

"How could you have fucked this up so completely?" the Youngstown Steel president asked his security chief.

"How was I supposed to stop the wuss from writing that shit?" Russo responded defensively.

Without dignifying the response, Landry turned to his son-in-law, the vice president of marketing.

"Our security chief apparently thinks that there was nothing he could do to prevent a story where our employees all but accuse the company of murdering the supervisor of our Brier Hill plant. You're an attorney, Landon. What defense would you suggest for Mr. Russo?"

"Temporary insanity?" Daumbrelle offered.

"Temporary insanity. Yes, that's good. Might I suggest another: conscious incompetence," Landry responded.

Now offended, Russo further exposed his hatred of his boyhood neighbor. "What did you want me to do? Kill the wuss after our meeting at Epperson's cottage?"

"Kill him? Did I say anything about murder, Landon?" Landry turned again to his son-in-law. "Mr. Russo seems to think he can solve problems by killing people, which is why we're in this mess. Perhaps he should consider doing his job."

"And what job is that?" Russo asked.

"The job of providing security at our plants. Did you even consider preventing our employees from shutting down operations, organizing a protest inside our plant, and then walking off our property with our equipment—company-issued hard hats that had been defaced and thrown into the Mahoning River?"

"I guess not."

"You guess not? If you had done your job, Mr. Russo, you would have made certain that our employees remained on their jobs and stayed in the mill until the end of their shift, which is 3:00 p.m., three hours *after The Examiner's* final deadline. There would not have been an organized protest, Lou Epperson would not have been elevated to a martyr, the company would have been spared the embarrassment of being accused of murder, and all of Youngstown wouldn't be conspiring against us. In short, your friend, the wuss, wouldn't have had a story. And I wouldn't be firing paper airplanes at your head."

Finished embarrassing Russo, Landry turned to the greater fool in the room. "Landon, what is your assessment of the damage?"

"Well, obviously, we've got a PR problem, but this was never going to be a walk in the park," Landon explained. "We can tidy things up with a response to *The Examiner*, deny any involvement in Epperson's death, and discredit Maier by picking apart his story. I'll call Annie Przybylski."

"And how has that worked out so far?" Landry asked rhetorically, dressing down the vice president who managed marketing. "Now, listen and learn."

Landry picked up the remaining scrap of the tear sheet on his desk, crumpling it in his hands.

"If you want to compromise a newspaper, you don't call the news department. You call the advertising department. Here's what you're going to do. You're going to call the advertising department and place $250,000 in advertising, starting with a full-page open letter to the community. The publisher will figure he's died and gone to heaven. I'll call him and introduce him to hell."

"Hell is a $250,000 ad buy?" Daumbrelle asked, dumbfounded.

"Hell is what I make it," Landry explained. "Hell for a newspaper publisher is losing a quarter-million-dollar account. I'll inform the publisher that I'll cancel the ad campaign if *The Examiner* doesn't play ball with us. That should disabuse him of any confusion about what his newspaper stands for."

"What about Maier?"

"We discredit every story he writes. The publisher will have a $250,000 incentive to muzzle him. Maier will suffer a bout of righteous indignation. He will be compelled to make a scene. For that, he will be fired or quit."

"Not soon enough."

"Perhaps, but let's remember to keep our eyes on the ball. Our goal is to execute the merger, escape from this godforsaken town, and return to New Orleans with dignity and grace. With the exception of our public interest campaign in *The Examiner*, there will be no communications with the media. Maier will not have access to any evidence that can disrupt the merger. Is that clear, Mr. Russo?"

"Perfectly," C. J. Russo said, ripping apart the paper airplane in his hands.

Landry closed the conversation with a familiar word: "Yes."

TWIST OF THE WIND

In Youngstown, smokestacks reached skyward like the arms of God. Steelworkers followed the smoke to the heavens. Work was fraught with danger and uncertainty. Accidents lurked in dark and perilous places. Disputes over working conditions and compensation were commonplace. Steel families prepared for accidents, strikes and shut-downs that left them without income to meet mortgage payments or to pay the doctor bills. They accepted weeks of hardship in return for the presumed certainty of a job.

Nothing had shaken the certainties of Steel Town more than the unexpected closing of the Campbell Works. Five thousand jobs were eliminated in one brief announcement. Those who lost their jobs didn't know how to react. Sixty thousand other steelworkers braced for inevitable. Youngstown had just lost its point. Steel Town called the day "Black Monday."

Lou Epperson's sudden and mysterious death stoked Youngstown's confusion. Revered by steelworkers throughout the Steel Valley, the Timekeeper was a workingman's hero who repre-sented the craft and culture of steelmaking. His death, inexplicably followed by the Campbell Works closing, was a one-two gut punch that left steelworkers confronting the stages of grief.

The first was denial. Many believed the news about the Timekeeper and the Campbell Works was somehow wrong. They clung to the false, preferable reality that their current condition of joblessness was temporary and that Youngstown would, as always, return to the turbulent normalcy of unpredictable employment passed from one generation to the next.

The second stage was anger. Steel Town was angry. It hated the current crop of managers at Youngstown Steel, the corporate interlopers from New Orleans who displaced local ownership, disdained the rough-and-tumble culture of an industrial city, and ran the company into the murky Mahoning River. Steel Town was looking for a fight. But first, the third stage of grief—depression—took hold.

How do I feel? How am I supposed to feel?

All of Youngstown considered the questions in Jordan Meier's story. One steelworker had expressed the sudden emptiness of an entire community.

Denial, anger, depression, and acceptance—the stages of grief are not linear. There's no predictable progression of the common experiences for the bereaved. On Black Monday, Youngstown throbbed with pain. There was no medicine, no counseling, and no prayer that could make it go away.

* * *

The steel priest felt the pain acutely. Father Ray worked in Youngstown steel mills before he was called to the ministry. But now, when it mattered most, words and faith eluded him. He felt inadequate, lost. What has a priest to say about a martyred saint who did not embrace religion?

The walking dead stirred throughout the union hall, lingering near an empty chair that was set next to a podium. A hard hat and a pair of steel-toed work boots were set on the floor next to the chair. The room drew silent as Father Ray rose to speak.

"Why me, God?" he asked. "That's the question all of us are asking, isn't it? That's the question you're asking me.

"Why me, God? I don't have an answer. I can't even think of an appropriate prayer to console you. Perhaps it is because we are also asking, 'Why Lou?' He is our friend, our brother. What explains the improbable accident that killed him? Did he die so that we could discover a larger truth? As a Catholic, I understand a story such as that one. Perhaps there is an answer in it.

"But I do not understand Lou Epperson's death. I do not understand what happened today. I do not accept. How could a company take everything so suddenly and without warning? How could that be right? How could it be just?

"A company is not human. It has no heart, no soul, no conscience. But it is not without sin. And for its sins, there will be retribution.

"I am but a parish priest. This is my prayer. This is my confession. I leave you in communion with each other."

"Send them to hell," came the shout from the union hall. The shout became a chant that overtook the hall.

"Be cool!" a strapping black man wearing a Local 2332 baseball cap shouted to the angry brotherhood. "Let's be cool, and remember why we're here. We're here for Lou."

Shouts and murmurs came back. To calm the crowd, Jonny Mann nodded to twenty-two men behind him. Each wore dark dress slacks, white shirts, black ties, and yellow hard hats. Youngstown Steel's Men of Steel Choir began to sing:

> Mine eyes have seen the glory of the coming of
> the Lord.

They sang through the second verse before finishing with the familiar "Glory! Glory! Hallelujah!" chorus of "The Battle Hymn of the Republic."

> I have read a fiery gospel writ in burnish'd rows
> of steel,
> As ye deal with my contemnors, so with you my
> grace shall deal;
> Let the Hero, born of woman, crush the serpent
> with his heel
> Since God is marching on.

The room grew quiet as Mann—millwright, electrician, crane operator, and a brother—came to the podium.

"This is a terrible day," Mann said. "But it is not our day. We are soldiers. Sometime soon, I am going to ask you to join me in battle. But not just now. Now I'm going to ask you to think about our brother, Lou Epperson.

"Lou was my friend, my guide. He found me shoveling slag into a blast furnace in Gadsden, Alabama, brought my family and me to Youngstown. Who does that for a black man from the South? We worked side by side in every dark corner of Campbell and Brier Hill. He taught me how to run the overhead crane. One wrong move, and I snap off the fingers of a loader. Move the crane too suddenly, and I drop twenty tons of steel in the warehouse, maybe crushing the men beneath.

"Look out for your brother, he taught me. So I look out.

"No one knew the mills like Lou. But the company tells us he was killed in an industrial accident. That is an impossibility, a lie. Another lie from a company that wants to shut us down, eliminate our jobs, kill the town just like they killed Lou."

The brotherhood went into a frenzy. They chanted, "Lou. Lou. Lou."

Jonny Mann ended the chants by raising his arms to the sky. "Let's take a moment to honor our brother. Lou Epperson was a spiritual man, not a religious one. Stand with me, and honor him in the way that has the most meaning to you. You can say a prayer or just honor him with your thoughts."

He ended the silence with a tribute of solidarity: "We are with you, Lou." Then he called LouAnn Epperson to the podium.

LouAnn rose from her chair and walked to the podium in the union hall.

"My father is an agnostic," LouAnn began her eulogy. "He believes that nothing is known or can be known of the existence or nature of God or of anything beyond material phenomena. He claims neither faith nor disbelief in God.

"I use the present tense because I believe—he believes—that existence is eternal. 'This is not the best of all worlds,' is what he said to me when I struggled with the death of my mother. You've heard him say that, too, perhaps as you explained your own struggles to him. This is not the best of all possible worlds.

"We traveled to Japan after I graduated from college. It was as much a research expedition as it was a rite of passage. As engineers, we were fascinated by the new technologies that Japanese companies were creating to move out of an industrial era that limited their culture and their understanding of the world. As tourists, we traveled to Mt. Fuji, an active volcano that is one of Japan's three sacred mountains. Our pilgrimage took us to Aokigahara, a spiritual forest at the base of the mountain.

"Aokigahara has been called the perfect place to die. More than five hundred people have ended their lives amid its Sea of Trees. My father found solace in this place that spooked others. Listening to the sounds that echoed through the trees, he discovered *kodama*, the spirits in Japanese folklore that inhabit the trees.

"When we returned to Youngstown, my father would not speak of our journey. He considered it sacred. I think he saw the coming darkness, the struggle that he would have in his relationship to the divine. It was then I realized that I was on my own.

"There are spirits, too, in the dark forest of steel mills along our polluted river. We hear them in the combustion of the blast furnaces. We feel them when molten iron is poured from a transfer ladle. We see them as red-hot pipes shoot across the floor. And we join them in the smoke that wafts through the smokestack toward the heavens.

"There's a long poem about our spirits. It's called 'Smoke and Steel' by Carl Sandburg. Here in Youngtown, amid our Sea of Trees, I'd like to read the opening passage:

"Smoke of the fields in spring is one.

"Smoke of the leaves in autumn another.

"Smoke of a steel-mill roof or a battleship funnel.

"They all go up in a line with a smokestack.

"Or they twist...in the slow twist...of the wind."

After the memorial service, the Timekeeper's brothers filed past the empty chair next to the hard hat and steel-toed work boots. Some paused for a silent prayer. Others removed their watches, leaving them on an empty chair in symbolic tribute.

MISDIRECTION

LouAnn Epperson was well known to the steelworkers who worked the mills in Youngstown. Lifelong millwrights whose lives had been destroyed, or were about to be destroyed, approached her to express their grief and their fears. They saw her as one of the city's daughters and sons who would be forced to abandon their legacy to find a more fulfilling life in a time after steel.

"Perhaps he mentioned me," said the man wearing the Local 2332 baseball hat.

"All the time, Jonny," LouAnn answered. "My dad used to tell me how you'd steer that crane over the vast shipping warehouse with the precision of a surgeon, then drop the grappling hooks precisely between the pallets of those steel plates."

"He was a boss. I was union. We managed to stay friends. That doesn't happen anymore."

"He respected you immensely, Jonny," LouAnn said. "He called you 'The Man.'"

Jonny took the compliment and then stumbled for words.

"I don't know exactly how to put this…I worked with him on a project that was our secret. I didn't think much about it until you mentioned your trip to Japan."

"I don't understand," said LouAnn.

"Lou made a big deal of it, taking his kid, you, to Japan for graduating college. He was very proud of you. But the Japan thing wasn't very popular with the bosses or the boys in the mill, with Japan dumping its steel, ruining the American auto industry and all.

We just figured Lou was going to Japan to learn how the Japs made steel cheaper than we can."

"That was my dad," LouAnn acknowledged. "But we didn't visit any steel mills in Japan."

She described how they walked around Akihabara, known as Electric Town, where the buildings were covered in lights and signs flashed messages in vertical characters that they couldn't understand. It seemed that everyone carried a camera or a device that played music. Every shop in Akihabara sold the devices.

"The Japanese weren't secretive about their technologies," LouAnn continued. "In fact, they were quite proud of them, happy to flaunt them. Lou arranged for us to visit development labs—Sony, Panasonic, Canon, JVC—where the Japanese were making small cameras that didn't require film and video cameras that would record events on a cassette. You didn't need a big studio. All you needed was a small recording camera and a tabletop machine to play the recording. The Japanese companies seemed humbled by our curiosity. They gave us equipment you couldn't get in the US."

"That may explain these," said Jonny. He opened up a metal-dome lunch box and pulled out several pages of folded, hand-drawn schematics. "Your dad asked me to give them to you if anything happened to him. I figured the company wouldn't look for them in my lunch box."

"What are we looking at?" asked Jordan.

LouAnn, the engineer, needed only a few seconds to understand what she was seeing. "These are plans for the installation of a remote-powered video camera on an overhead crane. Look at the documents about the camera. They're in Japanese."

"Holy shit," said Jordan.

"There's more," LouAnn continued. "The first page is an electrical plan. It shows how to power-on the camera from a remote switch in the shipping office.

"That's Lou's office," Jordan observed.

"Brilliant, Sherlock," LouAnn acknowledged. "An electrical line runs from his office, up a steel beam to the underside of the crane, about forty feet overhead. My father could power-on the camera from his office."

"So the camera is in a position to record activity in the shipping yard?" Jordan asked. "The company said Lou was killed in an industrial accident—that he slipped and fell into the pit. But the embalmer at the funeral home said the force from a slip wouldn't kill him. Might knock him out. Leave him with a concussion or a nasty headache. But a fatal blow from a slip by a guy who knew the mill like the back of his hand? Unlikely. The video might show us what really happened."

Jonny Mann reigned in the speculation with a reality check:

"I don't mean to pee on your parade, but it is unlikely the camera was operating. Lou used it for security and inventory monitoring. I'd make a pass of the warehouse after my shift to document changes in inventory—stacks of steel plates that were either higher or lower following a shift. Or possible safety problems, like debris on the floor between the plate stacks. We looked for unsafe stacks that may have shifted or might be leaning. But someone had to turn the camera on, and someone had to remove the cassette from the camera.

"I can tell you two other things about the camera," Jonny explained. "I helped Lou install it. We were the only two who know about it, at least until now. The bad news is that there is no way to retrieve it without attracting attention. The shipping yard at Brier Hill is still operating. I'm scheduled for a shift in my crane there tomorrow. There will be security everywhere. Anyone who knows about the camera—that would be us—would lead the company straight to it."

Now less enthusiastic about uncovering a clue in Lou Epperson's mysterious death, Jordan confronted the obvious problem. "So we don't know what's on a recording on a Japanese video camera that Lou and Jonny installed without the knowledge of the company. We can't even get a look at it."

LouAnn thought about her father. He would see the obstacles as a test, a puzzle that could be solved by putting random pieces in a predetermined place.

"I know my father," LouAnn said. "We can make some reasonable assumptions. First, he had information that was damaging to the company. Second, he knew they would find out about it. Third, he anticipated that they might harm him to prevent him from blowing the whistle. Fourth, he left us clues to solve his murder, unravel a mystery, and maybe save the town. So let's get our hands on that camera."

"And I thought this was going to be hard," Jordan sneered.

"Seriously, this could be a dangerous task, LouAnn," Jonny warned. "If anyone figures out what we're up to, we'll lose our jobs. Maybe get hurt."

"Then count me in," Jordan volunteered. "I hate the graveyard shift."

"We still have the problem of access," Jonny said. "We can't get to the camera without leading the company straight to evidence that might be recorded. Maybe I sneak around the plant, climb up to the cab, and remove the cassette from the camera. But that was before the company announced the closing of the Campbell Works. Not now. Security is tight. They know we're on to them. Everyone is watching. I wouldn't know how to get the video out of the plant and past the gate."

"Maybe we can sneak in," Jordan offered.

Mann was skeptical. "You're the reporter who wrote the story about Lou in *The Examiner* aren't you?"

"That's me," Jordan replied.

"Nice story, but you can't just sneak in and out of that mill unnoticed, college boy," Jonny said. "Leave the messy work for the mill hunks."

LouAnn was way ahead of the emerging plan, thinking like her father, a steelworker. "That sleazy security chief will be watching our every move," she reasoned. "Let's use that to our advantage. Jonny, can you get one of the brothers in under the radar? Operations as usual. A little misdirection perhaps?"

Jonny Mann thought for a moment. "Yah, I've got just the man."

"Good," said LouAnn. "One other request: do you have a mailing package and a few stamps around here?"

"Got 'em in the office,"

"So we're going to bring down Youngstown Steel by mail?" Jordan asked.

"Something like that," LouAnn replied, her mind already processing the next move.

DEMONS

The demons took C. J. Russo back to Roslyn Avenue and the horrific November morning that brought his father and younger brother to their fate. An explosion. The sickening confusion of debris, blood, and body parts. Familiar faces transformed into grotesque figures. The recurring nightmare shook the security chief at Youngstown Steel from his sleep. Tortured again, he cursed the demons for letting him live.

Russo took the latest nightmare as a warning. Hours earlier, Jennings Landry reminded him that unintended consequences from unforeseen circumstances would not go unpunished. Landry sounded like his father, the small-time gangster-punk known as Cadillac Charlie, who would humiliate him just for being his son. Now his boss, the Youngstown Steel president, blamed Russo for events beyond his control: the screwup with the Timekeeper, the accusations by a smart-ass daughter, and a city riled up over a fucking newspaper article. And then there was Jordan Maier. Russo hated the sniveling boyhood neighbor—the wuss—for witnessing his family's humiliation so long ago. Now he resented him for stirring up a mess.

The demons kept C. J. awake. He rolled over the events, again and again, in his mind: *That* morning on Roslyn Avenue. His involvement in the Timekeeper's murder at Brier Hill. Steelworkers marching out of the Campbell Works and tossing their hard hats into the river. The demons. He must make them go away.

An unanticipated thought brought him to full consciousness. Something hidden at the Brier Hill Works linked him to terrible events. C. J.'s survival depended on finding the incriminating evidence and burying it. To do so, he had to outmaneuver a ghost.

Demons be damned. Russo headed to the shipping mill at the Brier Hill Works before dawn broke.

With the graveyard shift suspended, the inside of the mill looked like a dark cathedral from Dante's *Inferno*. Shadows reflected off the soaring, stained black walls. As morning arrived, daylight streamed through the windows on the mill's roof, sending shafts of light down to the warehouse floor. The light illuminated the rows of stacked steel plates. Russo shuddered at the illusion: tombstones.

The morning light also revealed a solitary figure moving between the tombstones. It was Hoppy Crawford, the marginally illiterate handyman who roamed through the Brier Works like a mouse.

Hoppy's existence was well known to steelworkers and management at the Brier Hill Works. By most accounts, he lived in the tool room near the motor pool, never punching a time card, bunking in a cot, washing occasionally in the shipping yard locker room, and sucking down canned Chef Boyardee from a vending machine in the commissary. Hoppy was periodically seen leaving the Brier Hill Works in a beater and an old Youngstown Steel tool truck that he kept running.

Hoppy's nominal job was fixing small equipment. He moved randomly through all the mills, tool belt hanging under his skinny ass, fixing small motors, broken equipment, and worn-out machines. Russo paid no attention to the mouse as he approached.

"Lookin' fer sumpin, boss?" Hoppy asked with a toothless grin.

"Mind your business, hillbilly," Russo replied, brushing past him as a legion of steelworkers began arriving for the morning shift at the Brier Hill Works.

Slinking away, Hoppy disappeared into the chaos of the shift change as steelworkers manned their equipment, causing their machines to roar. On a mission to find and bury evidence, Youngstown Steel's security chief never noticed the cassette that was stashed in Hoppy Crawford's tool belt.

Russo was immediately distracted by the arrival of the day's workforce. The steelworkers all donned the same work clothes—dark gray Dickies pants and shirts with their regulation yellow hard hats. Each steelworker toted a metal-dome lunch pail. Russo dismissed the uniform as a harmless tribute to the Timekeeper. The show of unity, though, had another effect: it made the shift workers indistinguishable from each other. Together, they blended into a mass of gray and yellow.

Okay, assholes, you want to play? I can play too.

Russo decided to station himself in Lou Epperson's office. Though he doubted a new search would yield new clues, he took the office apart again, just as he had done a few days earlier. The same inventory logs kept in the steel desk. Nothing more.

Must think like the Timekeeper. What was his evidence? For what was he willing to die?

Whatever it was, Russo was convinced that it was hidden in a place the Timekeeper knew inside-out—the mill. He sat back in Lou Epperson's chair and decided to adapt the traits of the Timekeeper: look and discover. He had a hunch that a hidden truth would be revealed and that Epperson's unpleasant daughter and her wuss of a boyfriend were desperate to uncover it.

I'm watching now, assholes.

It took time, nearly the entire eight-hour shift, to put the pieces together.

As Russo watched from Lou Epperson's office in the warehouse, shipping operations ran routinely. An operator maneuvered an overhead crane over palettes of steel plates, dropping clawlike hooks from the underside of the carriage. Thirty feet below, crews signaled the operator to position the carriage and the hooks at precise vertical and horizontal positions. Once in position, the crews would insert the hooks between palettes then signal the operator to lift the tons of steel plates. The operator would then maneuver the cab to a dock where a load was set on a railcar or flatbed tractor-trailer.

The process was repeated as long as there were railcars and trucks to load. Due to the skill of the crane operator, accidents were rare—except when a crew member caught his glove between a hook and a plate, usually resulting in snapping off a finger. Occasionally, entire loads would slip unexpectedly from the hooks, dropping tons of steel on the warehouse floor. Steelworkers caught under the plates were killed instantly, organs crushed under the weight. It would take hours to lift the plates, scattered like pick-up sticks, off the bodies.

Watching the shipping operation for the first time, the security chief was impressed by the skills of the crane operator and his obvious concern for safety. Such a man might be useful. Russo opened the file cabinet in Lou Epperson's office and quickly found the operator's name in the personnel file:

> **Jonny (not Johnny) Mann**
> Hiring date: October, 17, 1962
> Millwright, 10-17-1962 to March 25, 1965
> Electrician, March 27, 1965
> Overhead crane operator, 3-25-65–present
> Crane Operation Certification YS298498500 BHW
>   5-20-67; Renewal, 7-2-75
> Hired by: Lou Epperson, BHW superintendent
> Address: 167 Liberty Street, Girard, Ohio 44420
> Call for emergency: 330-747-0625
> Auto tag: YS-BHW-S-726 1970 Ford pickup
> Race: African-American
> Education: High school (GED), State of Alabama
> Medical: No impairments
> Affiliations: Shop steward, USW Local 2332
> Citations: Accused of off-work alcoholism
> (File: MANN-9-21-72)
> DISMISSED PER YS INVESTIGATION AND VOUCHER
> FROM PLANT SUPERINTENDENT LOU EPPERSON

Known to frequent Golden Dawn Tavern following his shifts

The alarms in C. J. Russo's suspicious brain went off as he reached the bottom of the personnel file. An alcoholic union sympathizer hired and trained by the Timekeeper himself was operating the overhead crane in the shipping department. Russo didn't think he was there just to move steel.

Known to frequent Golden Dawn Tavern…

Flipping through the personnel file, Russo accidentally dropped it on the floor. As he crawled under the desk to retrieve it, he discovered something equally suspicious: a push-button switch connected to an electrical line. Russo traced the wiring along the wall of the office and out to the shipping yard floor. He followed it to a pillar and then to the beams supporting the overhead crane one hundred feet away. When his eyes reached the cab of the crane, he spotted it: a box welded to the bottom of the cab. Russo could also make out the broad features of the black man in the cab of crane. Mann. Jonny Mann.

Confused, Russo returned to Lou Epperson's office near the far end of the shipping warehouse.

What's with the wire? Is Mann an accomplice? What was Lou Epperson up to?

Then it came to him. Russo had removed an unfamiliar machine from the Epperson cottage—some kind of Japanese gizmo. A video cassette player? That means that…

Shit.

Russo pressed the button on the underside of the Timekeeper's desk just as the siren marking the end of the day shift blared through the Brier Hill Works. He scampered outside the office to see if he had activated the camera on the underside of the overhead carriage and to confront Jonny Mann.

Mann was already headed out of the plant. He climbed down from his perch above the shipping yard to join several hundred of his brethren—all dressed in gray Dickies, wearing yellow hard hats, and carrying metal-dome lunch pails—as they walked en masse out the gate. Amid the crowd, one steelworker thrust his arm upward, above the sea of hard hats, displaying a video cassette.

Unable to reach Mann and the elusive cassette, trapped amid his enemies, C. J. Russo confronted demons once more.

BRIER HILL PIZZA

Brier Hill pizza is Youngstown's signature dish. With origins in the Basilicata region of Italy, it was perfected in the neighborhood where poor Italian immigrants established a community on a hillside above a steel mill. The immigrants cleared thorns and coal from the hillside to plant small yard-gardens that grew sweet Roma tomatoes, bell peppers, and Genovese basil. After harvesting, the vegetables and herbs were reduced in a Sunday sauce that simmered for hours, creating a distinctive aroma that wafted through neighborhoods. Sunday sauce was ladled over hand-tossed dough, baked, and then topped with sliced peppers and grated Pecorino Romano cheese instead of the more typical mozzarella slices. Youngstowners believe you can't truly understand the city without appreciating the ingredients that make its pizza so special.

C. J. Russo followed his nose. Jonny Mann's personnel file provided the scent: *Known to frequent Golden Dawn Tavern following his shifts.*

Losing Mann in the monochromatic mass exodus from the Brier Hill Works, Russo headed to The Golden Dawn, the neighborhood tavern just outside the gate of the Brier Hill Works. Russo slipped unnoticed into a secluded booth in a back corner, removed from the bar, of the crowded tavern.

The bar was bustling at the end of the day shift. Jordan Maier and LouAnn Epperson were seated there, backs to Russo's line of site. Like the other patrons, mostly steelworkers who had finished their shifts at the plant, Jordan wore the uniform of the day: work boots

94

and the gray Dickies work wear. As with the other customers, he kept his yellow Youngstown Steel hard hat on his head.

Jonny Mann arrived a few minutes later carrying his lunch pail. He took the barstool next to Jordan and placed his pail on the floor next to the stool. Jordan reached down and pushed it under his own seat. After the exchange was complete, Russo made his move.

"You know what's really funny?" Russo said as reached Jordan and LouAnn. "You two think you are so smart."

Jordan extended an invitation he knew would be refused. "We were about to order beer and pizza. Want to join us, C. J.?"

"Sorry to ruin your meal, wuss," Russo responded. "I think I'll just see what's in that lunch pail."

Russo picked the pail from the floor, placed it on the bar, and opened it. He pulled out a peanut butter and jelly sandwich and a banana. Then a cassette.

"I think I'll just feast on this," he said, waving the cassette. Mann acted outraged. "You have no authority to take our stuff. We're in a tavern, not on company property. It's none of your business."

"I'm making it my business," Russo said. "You just removed company property from a Youngstown Steel plant."

"What are you going to do? Arrest me?" Mann taunted.

"No, but I can have you fired," Russo responded. "For now, I think I'll watch a video. Good luck on the unemployment line."

"Eat me," Mann snarled as Russo left the bar with the cassette in hand.

C. J. Russo figured he had cleaned up the mess. He held in his possession the hidden video that implicated him and Landon Daumbrelle in Lou Epperson's murder. A dead whistleblower could not scuttle a corporate merger without evidence.

Russo headed to Youngstown Steel headquarters to celebrate his triumph. He arrived in Jennings Landry's office, where the Japanese videocassette player taken from the Epperson cottage had been jerry-rigged to a television monitor.

"It took us hours to figure out this Japanese gizmo," Landry explained. "I want you to know, Mr. Russo, I had complete faith that you would acquire the content that apparently makes this foreign device so important to our interests."

Landry pulled a bottle of bourbon from his desk. "I think we'll forego the boilermakers today," he said, pouring drinks.

"To movie night," Landon Daumbrelle said, raising his glass in a toast.

"To the future," Landry corrected, touching his glass to his son-in-law's.

"Hold on, gentlemen," Russo warned. "What you see next may be shocking, but it saves our asses. I give you the real death of the Timekeeper."

Russo turned on the TV and popped the cassette in the player. The TV screen turned dark as the video began to roll. Japanese letters appeared, followed by the fuzzy image of a small Japanese woman in a kimono. She removed the kimono and started touching herself. She was soon joined by a naked Japanese man who began fondling her.

Transfixed, Landry could barely form words. "What is this, some kind of joke?" he finally asked.

"There must be some mistake," Russo protested.

"Mistake? Yes, dear boy, a rather graphic one," Landry said with unmistakable contempt.

As usual, Landon Daumbrelle missed the point. "Can I keep it?" he asked.

An angry and embarrassed Russo mocked the marketing executive with an explicit hand gesture at the zipper of his pants.

Daumbrelle was unfazed by what he realized was a bad idea. "I was just suggesting that we might discredit Lou Epperson by tracing pornography back to him," he explained.

Meantime, Landry was pouring himself another bourbon. "How ni-*ice*," he drawled, recalling the twisted story from LouAnn Epperson. "I'm trying to salvage the steel industry and escape this rotting shithole of a town, but I have put my fate in the hands of a pervert and an incompetent gangster."

Silently, the three conspirators considered how they had been played. Throwing back his bourbon, Youngstown Steel's president broke the silence with words that succinctly described his predicament. "I am so fucked," he said.

* * *

The pizza arrived with a second pitcher of beer at The Golden Dawn.

Jonny Mann recounted how Hoppy Crawford skulked his way into the Brier Hills Works an hour before the start of the day shift, removed a video cassette from a Japanese camera mounted on an overhead crane, walked it out of the steel mill, placed it in an addressed mailing packet, and mailed it to California.

"Brilliant plan, Jonny," LouAnn proclaimed.

"All I did was pack a lunch and bait that snake," he replied. Mann described how he put the Japanese porn video—a gag gift to the boys in the mill from Lou Epperson's Japan excursion—into his lunch pail along with his lunch, two peanut butter and jelly sandwiches and a banana.

"I just climbed into my crane with my lunch pail and pretended like I didn't see Russo watching me," he explained. "I ducked down to fiddle with the camera box on the underside of my cab, but Hoppy had already made off with the goods. Russo had no idea.

"Then it was work as usual. Hoisted tons of steel with my crane during my shift in the plate mill. I should have dropped a load of steel plates on that asshole's head, but that would have taken the fun out of it. Thought about it, though, as I ate one of my peanut butter and jelly sandwiches up there in the cab."

Mann laughed heartily. "Like I said, he took the bait," he explained to Jordan and LouAnn. "Russo had his security flunkies follow the two of you to The Dawn. You led him right to the switcheroo."

"I can't believe he had us followed. Then he hid in that corner booth," Jordan said. "The lunch pail switch was epic."

Jordan then broke into his best C. J. Russo imitation. "You know what's really funny? You two think you are so smart," he smirked in a dead-on mimic. "I can't believe he said that."

"I can't believe you invited him to stay for pizza," LouAnn added.

"Not just any pizza," Jonny corrected, "Brier Hill pizza." Turning serious, LouAnn pulled her father's Tramway from her pocket and looked at the time. "Just about now, our video is on its way to Pasadena," she said. "And just about now, C. J. Russo, Landon Daumbrelle, and Jennings Lambert are sitting in an office at Youngstown Steel headquarters watching a Japanese porn film, trying to understand how everything went so wrong."

"Do you think Lou somehow set all this in motion?" Jordan asked.

"All I know is that he would want you to have this," said LouAnn, handing Lou Epperson's treasured watch to Jordan. "Here's to time."

By the time on the Tramway, the steelworker, the reporter, and the Timekeeper's daughter spent the next two hours deriving the maximum enjoyment from pitchers of beer and Brier Hill pizza.

PART THREE

ABSOLUTION

THE SHRINE

As was her custom, Annie Przybylski arrived in the newsroom at 6:00 a.m. The steady managing editor appeared unfazed by the unforeseen events that had devastated the city and, more importantly to Annie, how *The Examiner* handled the story. This day, as with all others, she set her sights on the day ahead at the 7:00 a.m. news meeting with editors.

Annie was back in her space, secure in the familiarity of the newsroom. That is until she noticed the light filtering under the door of the Shrine. The office located in a dim corner of *The Examiner* newsroom had not been used in years. There was a reason. It was retired after the death of William Randolph Williamson, the flamboyant *Examiner* publisher who believed he was the second coming of William Randolph Hearst.

Annie's phone rang as if on cue. "Can we talk?"

The voice belonged to Junior—William Williamson Jr., the current publisher and son of the original. A 6:00 a.m. meeting with the publisher in the Shrine could only mean one thing: *Annie girl, you are about to be fired.*

It was the first time that anyone could recall the use of the Shrine. Shuttered on the day of Williamson Sr.'s death, all of the office's contents were left in place: the day's edition of *The Examiner* on his desk, the files on the conference table, the poured glass of brandy on the credenza, the photos on the mahogany paneling, and the toiletries in the adjoining private bathroom. The shutters on the office's windows were closed, never to be opened again.

All eyes on her, Annie strode across the envelope of light that escaped under the door of the Shrine.

Business as usual, show no emotion. I may be devastated, but I'll be damned if I show weakness to my staff.

The light from a solitary Tiffany lamp on the publisher's desk splashed out from the Shrine as Annie walked through the door that, for years, had been opened only by the maid who dusted the mausoleum and, now, by the son who preferred not to occupy it.

"Have a seat over there, Annie," Junior said, pointing to a place at the conference table. "I can't say that I like sitting behind my overbearing father's ego desk."

Annie sat at the table, waiting for Junior to join her before she spoke. "Let me make this easy for you, Bill," she said. "It's a pivotal time for the newspaper with everything that just happened. I understand if you think it's time for a new managing editor."

Junior saw where the conversation was headed. "You think I'm going to fire you?"

"Well…yes." Annie stammered.

Junior changed course. "Look at this room, will you? It's a relic. I never wanted it. I put my office downstairs next to the ad department. These days, being a publisher is all about sucking up to advertisers. This city needs something more."

"You mean you're not firing me," Annie asked.

"Of course not. This newspaper needs you and that young reporter, Maier."

"So this is a pep talk," Annie said.

"Not exactly," Junior explained. "I've sold the newspaper to Michael Panessa."

"The mall mogul?" she asked. She wanted to say "the sleazebag," but she kept her informed opinion to herself.

"That's the one," Junior said. "He's got the money and the grit for it. I don't anymore. I'm counting on you to make a difference with our journalism."

"My, but we've had our share of news recently," said Annie.

With that, the reluctant publisher and the reticent managing editor left the Shrine, never again to use the room.

FALL FROM GRACE

The managing editor's morning was already exhausting. She had visited the Shrine, learned *The Examiner* had been sold, lost her Jell-O publisher, and was introduced to a scary new boss. Worst of all, she wasn't fired. It was just 7:30 a.m. Time now to castrate a reckless reporter who had gone off the reservation.

Two days removed from acclaim, Jordan Maier spun a story that defied credulity, an adventure that liberated evidence presumed to explain the death of Lou Epperson. Maier contended that unseen, secret tapes implicated Youngstown Steel execs in a murder and a national conspiracy. Annie Przybylski was having none of it.

"Let's see if we can summarize the story of Jordan Maier's unscheduled day off, shall we?" Annie began without waiting for an answer. "You skip work to cavort with your girlfriend and her steelworker buddy, steal a Japanese video that belongs to Youngstown Steel, then gloat over pitchers of beer at The Golden Dawn. Even a reporter as inexperienced as you would have to agree that those are the pertinent facts of your adventurous day away from the office yesterday, a fair description of exploits better suited for *The Gong Show* than a credible newspaper."

"You don't get it, Annie. The video is a smoking gun," Jordan maintained.

"And just where is this smoking gun?" Annie asked.

"I think that it's about to arrive at Caltech."

"Ah, a secret, traveling smoking gun. A video is removed from a Japanese camera in a Youngstown steel mill, only to be delivered to a renowned university in Pasadena, California, presumably to prove that there is more to temporal existence than screwing around with inferior American technology. Is that your story?"

"Something like that," Jordan smirked.

"So where to for your next evidence? "Roswell, New Mexico?"

"This isn't science fiction, Annie. I'm chasing a big story. Bigger than Black Monday—"

Annie cut him off at the mouth. "Spare me your fantasies, Jordan. Here's the nonfiction version: theft, aiding, and abetting, transporting stolen property across state lines. God knows what else. Do you have any idea how many laws you may have broken? I should be calling the FBI instead of scolding you for ditching work, not to mention firing you for unethical journalistic conduct."

"Which is it then, Annie?" the impertinent reporter asked.

"I'm trying to decide," the steely managing editor answered. "Now get out of my office. I'm in no mood for this."

Jordan skulked out of Annie's office and into the newsroom, where a roomful of editors and reporters were already gossiping over the morning's dramas. Jordan could feel the hostility as he headed to his desk. "Dead man walking," he heard one of the eunuchs say.

An hour later, Jordan was summoned back to Annie's office. "Much as you are unable to fathom events that don't affect you personally, I've decided to allow you to redeem yourself," she said. "Now do yourself a favor, Jordan. Keep your mouth shut, listen, and do as I say."

Annie recounted her conversation with Junior in the Shrine and her subsequent telephone call with the new publisher.

"Panessa wants you to profile him for this Sunday's paper," she said wearily. "I think it's a bad idea, but I can't afford to fight him right from the start."

Jordan dismissed the assignment. "I'm covering other stories," he said.

"Not anymore," Annie shot back. "You are off the Epperson story. You are off the Youngstown Steel story. You will not win a Pulitzer Prize. You will, however, interview the new owner of *The*

Examiner about his plans. If you do not, I will fire you on the spot and report you to the authorities."

"Do I have a choice?" he asked cynically.

"Not unless you want to spend the rest of your career at an obscure country weekly interviewing farmers about a peanut that resembles Jimmy Carter. Here's Panessa's number. Now leave."

Launched into the stratosphere a few days earlier, Jordan Maier felt himself fall from the sky and from grace. He braced for a crash landing, wondering why Michael Panessa coerced Annie Przybylski into saving his sorry ass.

THE GROUND TOUR

Jordan had lost his story, his way, and nearly his job. The events of the previous twenty-four hours left him with a hangover, an upset stomach, and an unsettling premonition. Things would get worse.

Unable to push through the sickening feeling, he looked for a place to puke. He leaned over an *Examiner* newspaper box and proceeded to hurl behind the headlines. However allegorical, barfing failed to calm his nerves. He broke out in a sweat as his ride drew close. The black Lincoln Continental limo arrived on cue. Jordan took it for a hearse.

In a city where a wise guy could avoid a scheduled Youngstown tune-up by starting his car with remote-controlled ignition device, the Continental was the preferred vehicle for the Youngstown joyride. There were two doors on each side of the Continental. With the back doors hinged from the rear, the two doors opened from the middle to showcase the car's roomy interior.

In Youngstown, the Continental was more appreciated for a design flaw: the suicide doors, as car buffs called them. The suicide doors could open accidently, or not so accidentally, on the highway. Road wind would cause them to fling open, creating the same effect that unfurling the jib had on a sailboat—the vessel would swing in the wind. With the open side of the Continental exposed to the passing road, passengers were known to fall out of the moving vehicle. Or bodies were thrown from it.

Jordan was well aware of the Continental's reputation. He'd written a few obituaries of notorious Youngstowners who spent their final minutes riding in a luxury Continental.

Wearing a snappy chauffeur's cap and a waistcoat, Eddie Mancini emerged from the driver's seat of the Continental that had come for Jordan Maier. The slight and harmless-looking driver looked incapable of wheeling the yacht around, but he docked the boat so the starboard side faced his passenger. Still nauseous and wary of the young man behind the wheel, Jordan opened the suicide doors and took a seat inside the Continental.

It took the driver a minute to introduce himself. "I'm Captain Eddie. Eddie Mancini. Eddie the driver," he said.

God help me. I'll be spending the last minutes of my life on a Love Boat horror cruise.

The thought was unexpectedly reassuring. *How dangerous could Captain Eddie be?* Jordan thought he'd keep his last words friendly. "How's it going, Captain Eddie. I'm Jordan. Jordan Maier. Jordan the reporter."

Eddie liked the game. "Mr. Panessa, Michael Panessa, the boss, asked me to give you the ground tour," Eddie played, pleased with himself. "I've been assigned to bring you to him."

"How convenient. I've been assigned to interview him."

"Lucky you," Eddie said. He actually meant it. "I heard that the boss just bought *The Examiner*. I guess you work for him now."

"Lucky me."

Eddie had never met a reporter. He was nervous about talking to one. "Written anything important lately?" he asked.

"Not really. But I hope to."

"I guess reporters have to ask a lot questions."

"They do."

"I'm good at asking questions, but I'm better at driving cars. Anyways, I'm just glad I don't have to work in the mills. Too bad all those steelworkers lost their jobs. I read all about them in the newspaper."

"I read all about them in the newspaper too."

"That's a good one." Eddie laughed, enjoying the banter perhaps a little too much. "Mr. Panessa says I talk too much. He says my blabber can annoy the passengers. I'll shut up now and give you the ground tour."

"I like listening to you, Eddie. Keep talking as long as you want."

The Continental reached a shopping mecca that extended for blocks.

"That's Boardman Shopping Plaza. Mr. Panessa built it back in the fifties for all the families that drove to the suburbs in their cars," Eddie explained, sticking to a script he had rehearsed. Then he drove the Continental through a busy intersection to the boss's masterwork—Boardman Park Mall.

* * *

Few individuals had a more profound impact on American culture than Michael Panessa. Raised by an immigrant stepfather in a working-class section of Youngstown, Panessa became a civil engineer who pioneered plaza and shopping mall construction.

Boardman Park Mall, which opened in 1970, typified the malls that spread across the country during the era. Panessa clustered specialty shops around corridors leading to huge "anchor" stores such as Sears and Macy's that carried all the household necessities of suburban life. He was the first developer to put a roof over the stores and surround them with an ocean of parking. Panessa's malls quickly became the center of community life in suburbs from Cleveland to Tampa.

By 1977, Panessa's personal wealth was estimated at $1.4 billion. He was included on *Forbes* magazine's first list of richest Americans. Eddie wasn't supposed to say that. He was just supposed to extol the boss's wisdom.

"Mr. Panessa calls malls the new American cities," Eddie said, moving beyond his depth.

"Others see them as suburban monstrosities, Eddie." Jordan explained how Panessa's enclosed shopping centers were driving out family-owned businesses and destroying downtowns across the US.

"I wouldn't know about that," said the chauffeur.

As the tour headed into the final stretch. Eddie turned the Continental into a parklike campus with two modern buildings. Youngstown Steel's headquarters building was located on one side of a tree-lined boulevard, Pan American Development on the other. An array of fountains circled a large stainless-steel Unisphere separating the two buildings at a roundabout. The boulevard ended at an airstrip near the back of the property. Eddie dropped off his passenger near a Cessna parked outside the hangar.

"That's it for ground tour," Eddie announced. "Nice talking with you, Mr. Jordan the reporter."

Jordan was about to thank Captain Eddie for something—he was not sure for what—when a familiar man with a slight limp approached. Of all the people that Jordan neither wanted nor expected to see, C. J. Russo topped both lists. Jordan felt himself grow sick again. Then he identified the other man in his field of sight. He was wearing a white mechanic's jumpsuit, working on the engine of the Cessna. His black hair was slicked back, his features and mannerisms unmistakable.

Jordan's memory flashed to a horrific Sunday morning when a man in a mechanic's jumpsuit emerged from Cadillac Charlie's garage on Roslyn Drive: a boy, a ball, and imagination. *Wuss.* An explosion. Shards of metal and body parts. The bloody leg of Tommy Carabbiaat his side. A scream that overtook his consciousness.

Devastated by the summoning of ghosts from a traumatic day in his past, Jordan Maier puked again, violently, for the second time in an hour.

FEAR OF FLYING

Breeeeeeath.

Jordan was sitting in a folding chair, head in his hands, bent over, uncertain how he got here. Wherever *here* was.

The hazy environs slowly came into focus: maps on the wall, a two-way radio, and a metal desk. Michael Panessa materialized in the haze. He was sitting across from Jordan, sucking in air, then slowly expelling it, showing the reporter how breathing worked. C. J. Russo put a cup in the boss's outstretched hands as Panessa coached the panting reporter in the art of oxygen.

"Drink some water," Panessa instructed.

Jordan did. Rehydrating, he tried to put aside memory to deal with an unpleasant reality.

"I take it you have questions," Panessa offered. "Are you feeling well enough to ask them?"

"Where am I?" Jordan managed.

"'I'll take that as a yes. You're in an airplane hangar in Boardman."

"How did I get here?"

"Eddie brought you here."

"Eddie…oh yeah…I remember."

"See, we're making progress."

"Why did Eddie bring me here?"

Meaningless questions made Panessa impatient. "Is that the question you really want to ask me, son?" Panessa snarled.

Faculties returning, Jordan carefully considered what he was going to say next.

"Actually, no," he finally said. "What I really want to know is if you plan to kill me...because I'd rather you didn't."

"What a thing to say," Panessa said with a sly smile. "For a reporter of facts, you have quite an imagination, Mr. Maier. Do you have another, more pertinent question?"

Jordan looked straight at C. J. Russo: "Is *he* going to kill me?"

Panessa spun toward his associate. "Mr. Russo, are you going to kill Mr. Maier?"

"Not today," Russo said matter-of-factly.

"Good," Panessa said. "Our little reunion has left all of us a little worked up today. Perhaps we should return to our intended agenda. Now I have a question for you, Mr. Maier: Do you like to fly?"

"Not really."

"Don't worry. You'll be perfectly safe," Panessa explained.

"I'll be perfectly safe doing what?"

"Flying. You're going to accompany me on a short flight. When we're airborne, I'll provide the information for the story about me that you were assigned to write."

"What if I get airsick?"

"I don't think you can throw up any more than you already have," Panessa said.

"What the hell," Jordan said, following Panessa to the turboprop.

* * *

The noise from the Cessna was surprisingly minimal. With the propeller tips moving relatively slowly with a light load, the turboprop soared through the sky with a soothing hum. The plane was Michael Panessa's flying sanctuary. Even his nervous passenger had to admit that it was peaceful up there.

Just after takeoff, Panessa instructed Jordan to pay attention. The mall mogul took the plane south over Mill Creek Park, Youngstown's underappreciated Central Park. Following the park south until the green space ended in concrete and steel, Panessa took the Cessna over downtown, where the towering dark stacks of the steel mills rose along the Mahoning River. The plane turned east, following the river southeast toward Pittsburgh. Panessa turned the plane again at the spot where the Mahoning flowed into the Ohio River.

Then he turned the Cessna northwest, roughly paralleling the Ohio-Pennsylvania line. When the plane reached a point where Lake Erie dominated the horizon, Panessa turned the plane back toward Youngstown.

Not a word had been spoken since Jordan was instructed to pay attention. Panessa broke the silence with a test.

"What did you see?" he asked.

"I dunno. Roads, rivers, railroad tracks, steel towns, land, and a big lake."

"Good."

"You're messin' with me, aren't you?"

"I'll tell you what I saw: roads, rivers, railroad tracks, steel towns, land, and a big lake."

"Now I know you're messin' with me."

"Look more carefully," Panessa advised. "I see money. Big money."

Roads, rivers, railroad tracks, steel towns, land, and a big lake. Michael Panessa's next act could change the nation, perhaps even elevate him from forty-seventh place on the *Forbes* list of the richest men in the country.

He saw Youngstown as a national hub for American industry. All the materials required for America's mighty shipping, steel, auto, and construction industries were accessible. Panessa meant to connect them with a shipping lane that would connect Lake Erie to the Gulf of Mexico—Erie to the Mahoning, the Mahoning to the Ohio, the Ohio to the Mississippi, and the Mississippi to New Orleans. With the already navigable Ohio and Mississippi Rivers, nature had already created most of the shipping lane. All Panessa had to do was convince the federal government to dig a big ditch connecting Lake Erie at Ashtabula to the Mahoning in Youngstown—fifty-eight miles, just a few miles more than the Panama Canal.

Panessa's malls, which began in Boardman and spread to sub-urbs nationwide, served as proofs of concept. See the flow, make the deals, acquire property, develop the land, supply the equipment, pro-vide a destination, and command skilled workers—Youngstown had 30,000 of them. The newly unemployed and the soon-to-be unem-ployed would be available at discount wages. The nation's transpor-tation hub would come together at Pan America Park—the nation's central, industrial transportation hub in Youngstown.

Panessa could see the money flow from the hubs and spokes of industries converging at Youngstown. He calculated that his cut of shipping, trucking, cargo, property, and construction fees would triple his wealth. He just needed the federal government to finance building the canal, a small price to pay for sacrificing mills and jobs in Youngstown.

Jordan didn't know whether to find the vision brilliant or crazy. "That's the story the new owner of *The Examiner* wants me to write? I won't."

"Of course you will. You've already started," Panessa said, land-ing the Cessna at the Boardman airstrip.

Taxiing to the hangar, Panessa shut down the engine and remained in the cockpit, creating an awkward silence. Without the noise from the turboprop, the two men sat there, alone in the uneasy quiet. Maier grew increasingly uncomfortable as Panessa fell into deep thought, seemingly oblivious to his surroundings. His next words were astonishing.

"The weight of this sad time we must obey. Speak what we feel, not what we ought to say."

Jordan recognized the words immediately. "King Lear."

"The writer knows his Shakespeare," Panessa said. "I read your story in *The Examiner* called 'The Death of the Timekeeper.'" One does not often see Shakespeare cited in a news story. The reference was unexpected but relevant. You are to be congratulated for a meta-phor that most people in Youngstown would find obscure."

Panessa returned to Lear. "At this sad time we must obey, so we will speak what we feel, not what we ought to say." Then he tried to make Shakespeare relevant.

"You and I have unfinished business. You are wondering about an unpleasant day on Roslyn Avenue many years ago. You are wondering about the man at the scene. You are wondering what Mr. Russo is doing here. You are even wondering if I'm going to threaten you, coerce you, or whether I plan to kill you. I am going to answer these questions only once. What is said remains in the private confines of this cockpit. We shall never speak of them again."

"Let me start with Mr. Russo," Panessa continued. "Mr. Russo works for me, although the executives at Youngstown Steel may be surprised by that information. I have seen to his care since that terrible day on Roslyn Ave.

"As for me, I am not who you think I am. I am neither a murderer nor a hoodlum. I am a businessman, a very smart one. The fates of Youngstown now bring us together in a Shakespearean tragedy."

When Panessa finished speaking, Jordan confronted the question that tormented him: "And what is my role in this tragedy?" he asked.

"To write it," Panessa replied.

* * *

Taking his cue from his passenger, Eddie Mancini drove Jordan back to *The Examiner* in silence. Jordan needed to speak with LouAnn to recount the stories from a disturbing day, but his calls to the cottage went unanswered. In *The Examiner* newsroom, he finished his story on the grand vision of *The Examiner*'s new owner. Then he drove straight to the cottage.

The cottage, ransacked just a few days earlier, was put back together. LouAnn was nowhere to be found. Jordan found her note on the table beneath the mirror where the wooden cross was hung.

He opened the note tentatively and read:

Too many people have been hurt. I can only see more sadness here. It is more than I can bear. I'm returning to Pasadena to deal with the pain. Where are you, Billy Pilgrim?

ABSOLUTION

After six days, the sun emerged from the shadow of Black Monday. A morning breeze cleared the smoke from the Steel Valley, carrying the chill of autumn arriving. It was Sunday. Youngstown woke to the sound of church bells harmonizing with the muted echoes of machinery rumbling in the distance.

Landon Daumbrelle sat down for *eggs fauteux* and chicory-flavored coffee in the garden room of his suburban Youngstown home. The weekly indulgence transported him to Sunday brunch at Commander's Palace in New Orleans. There, he would dine leisurely while reading *The Times-Picayune*. Here, he substituted the local rag. Unfolding the Sunday morning edition of *The Youngstown Examiner*, his eyes found the front-page story on Michael Panessa written by Jordan Maier. Appetite gone and fantasy dashed, Daumbrelle washed down a disagreeable bite of pompano, poached eggs, and hollandaise with a bitter cup of coffee.

Michael Panessa returned to his sanctuary in the sky. He took the Cessna above the clouds, as close to heaven as he was cleared to go. At twelve thousand feet, where everything was comprehensible, the engine on the Cessna stalled. Rather than panic, Michael Panessa considered King Lear as he crashed into his kingdom.

C. J. Russo attended Mass at St. Anthony's Church in Brier Hill. During the liturgy, he reflected on a father and a brother killed in a horrible explosion. In prayer, he asked God why he had been spared. Taking confession for the first time as an adult, a priest absolved him of mortal sin.

Jordan Maier rose from a restless night on a blanket under a stand of trees at the cottage called Continuum. Wandering along Mosquito Lake in the light of the morning, he searched for someone he knew was no longer there.

LouAnn Epperson peered out the window of the 747 as the red-eye flight from Cleveland began its descent into LAX. Beyond the darkness, she could see the light of the horizon.

PART FOUR

SHE ARRIVES

TIME FLIES

Unlike the frantic trip that brought her home to grief and confusion, the red-eye back to LAX was routine and smooth. Only a few suits boarded the Boeing 747 for the 5:00 a.m. flight from Chicago that put them in downtown Los Angeles for the start of West Coast suit business. LouAnn purchased a business class seat in the all but empty upper cabin of the jumbo jet and settled in next to a window.

As the plane reached altitude, she tried sleep, but it did not come. It hadn't come for a week. Her mind raced alternately between emotion and attempts at reasoning. Her only reality: her father was gone forever. The hum of the jet engine and the gentle motion of plane brought a momentary sense of calm that only made her feel guilty. Somewhere over Nebraska, a voice caused her to open her eyes.

"Can't figure it out, kiddo?"

It was her father. He was sitting in the seat next to her.

"Daddy, is that you?"

"Of course it's me. Were you under the impression I had gone somewhere?"

"But they said you were…"

"Dead? I thought we had moved past that one."

"I have so many questions."

"Then ask the right ones."

"Why did you go?"

"That's not the right question."

"What's the right question?"

"That's for you to figure out."

Thoughts of the past week and future consequences raced through her mind: A shameless company cooks the books and commits fraud to justify an illegal merger. It eliminates a whistleblower who's ready to disclose the truth. The government is complicit, encouraging the conspiracy. An industry fundamental to the nation's economy is disrupted. It impacts economic stability and the balance of power. Thousands of workers lose their jobs. A city and its culture fall into demise and disarray. The industrial age ends. Social, economic, and political foundations teeter and fall.

"It's all too much. What can I possibly do?"

"Now that's the right question."

And then he was gone.

"Don't go," LouAnn pleaded.

"I'm right here," said the voice in her head.

LouAnn touched her forehead.

"This is where we solve the problem," the Timekeeper said. Then LouAnn put her hands over her heart.

"There is where we believe in each other," said her father.

"Forever?" asked LouAnn, touching her forehead with her finger, her other hand held over her heart.

"Always," said the voice of her father. Then he was gone.

LouAnn looked out the small window by her seat and watched, transfixed, as slices of the sky, wavering between light and darkness, passed by the window. In the transition to daylight, she stared at faint stars, which somehow seemed stationary even as the plane hurtled through the lower stratosphere of an orbiting Earth. Then came an epiphany: The airplane, an extension of man, is an innovation that changed transport and previous perceptions of the time it takes to travel. As perceived by stationary beings, the airplane disrupts the constancy of space. It creates an ever-changing reality affected by the motion and actions of humans and the machines they invented to move through it.

It was no accident that the Wright brothers were bicycle mechanics, LouAnn reasoned. Or that early airplanes seemed in some ways like bicycles. The transformations of technology have the character of organic evolution because all technologies are extensions of physical being. Here, humans, not technologies, control the direction of technological change.

The realization enabled LouAnn to understand her problem from a new and deeper perspective. Triggered by a key piece of unconsidered information—the passing sky as seen from a portal in an airplane traveling at five hundred miles an hour—LouAnn was able to apply her depth of prior knowledge into a leap of understanding: she could not fly into the future by applying the knowledge of bicycle mechanics. Rather, she could consider technological determinism as an extension of humans. Suddenly, she had a purpose: integrate knowledge to help people solve some of the world's most difficult and perplexing questions. She was heading in the right direction.

* * *

A third generation of computers had arrived, increasing the expanse of knowledge and the speed by which it could be distributed. These computers were suddenly portable and powerful, capable of being programmed by anyone with a basic knowledge of ones and zeros.

Most of the world's most exciting work in computer science and deterministic technology was occurring in California, not far from LouAnn's lab in Pasadena.

In Cupertino, a company called Apple, named after the fruit of Newton's formulation of the laws of motion and universal gravitation, introduced a personal computer for the mass market. The irony is that it would help disrupt the physicist's view of the physical universe that had dominated for three centuries.

In San Jacinto, engineers developed a scheme called ARCNET for managing line sharing among computer workstations and other devices connected by a local network.

In Redwood City, a company called Oracle was founded to develop database software and technology that stored and sorted enormous files of data and knowledge.

And at Caltech's Jet Propulsion Laboratory, engineers constructed and launched a deep space probe called Voyager 1 that would follow routine commands from NASA and return data from the farthest reaches of the solar system for nearly fifty years.

With technology advancing exponentially and data increasing by several magnitudes, an unlikely proposition was infused with possibility. LouAnn could not discount the expertise she acquired in computing and neuroscience at MIT. She had already established a reputation as an accomplished computer scientist.

Almost nothing had been invented yet. LouAnn considered the opportunity as the 747 started its descent into the half-light of a California morning. What a promising start.

SMUG

Three members of a secret society for women made their way to a basement lab in the Willis H. Booth Computing Center on the campus of the California Institute of Technology. Each had overcome the sexism in academia that excluded women from the fields of mathematics, engineering, the sciences, and the emerging specialty of computer science. Bonded by their gender and determined to amend the failures of academia, they came to the temple of techno-chauvinism to redesign the rules. At Caltech, they formed an exclusive society for visionary women in technology. They called it SMUG, short for Smart Unappreciated Gals.

Today, three members of SMUG gathered to offer condolences to the fourth member of the club. Or so they thought.

Christina Duncan and Aparna Singh arrived first. Both knew how to navigate the stately campus built for the male gods of science: the academic halls in the Spanish mission-style architecture of the Renaissance era, the Memorial Building inspired by the Taj Mahal, and the Athenaeum, the faculty boys' club named after Athena, the goddess of wisdom.

Duncan and Singh immediately appreciated the irony of their current location at Caltech: a basement.

Regarded as one of the world's best universities, perhaps *the* best for technology and science, Caltech collected Nobel laureates the way children in 1977 collected *Star Wars* action figures. Caltech brought planets, not mere mortals, to orbit its solar system.

Admittance to the exclusive club of science stars at Caltech required more than a beautiful mind, scientific achievement, and an exemplary curriculum vitae. Until 1955, you had to have testicles.

After getting her chemistry degree at Mount Holyoke and studying at MIT, Dorothy Ann Semenow was recruited to Caltech as the first graduate who was female. It took the intervention of Nobel laureate Linus Pauling to persuade the administration to rescind its rule prohibiting women from enrolling. Caltech made an exception for "women who give promise of great scientific contributions."

In 1955, Semenow became the first woman to earn a doctorate at Caltech. It took fifteen more years for Caltech to rescind its policy denying admittance to women as undergraduates. Twenty years after Dorothy Ann Semenow, Christina Duncan became the second woman to earn a doctorate at Caltech in 1975.

Two momentous events in 1977 caused Caltech to make the homogametic gender a permanent part of its chromosomes. The first was the sharp decline in American power and influence in the 1970s that caused the Department of Defense to develop new technologies to replace a military arsenal that had become obsolete. In 1975, Noah Altman, an inventor and electrical engineer who spent much of the decade in DOD overseeing research, was named director of the Defense Advanced Research Projects Agency in Arlington, Virginia. At DARPA, he discovered a self-assured intern with a master's degree in mechanical engineering from Virginia Tech. Her name was Christina Duncan.

Duncan's mantra of innovation and her criticism of military methods ruffled the uniforms at DARPA, where she was viewed as "that hippie girl who played video games on her computer." Altman saw something more. He arranged a secret grant at Caltech for Duncan to pursue nonlinear research untainted by military protocol, research that could guide the Pentagon to shifting its thinking about how to develop technology for military use.

There were no rules. Beyond a directive to restore military superiority that could take decades to achieve with traditional protocols, Altman encouraged Duncan to explore an innovation process of creative destruction where new technologies would quickly replace military hardware that had become obsolete, thus threatening national security.

The second event was NASA's mission to explore the outer reaches of the solar system. In 1936, the federal government set up the Jet Propulsion Lab at Caltech to build the rocketry that would later become the space program. JPL employed women as human computers, unheralded mathematicians who made calculations for male engineers. In the 1950s, women in the all-female computations group performed trajectory calculations using mechanical calculators. In 1961, it hired Dana Ulery as the first woman engineer to work alongside male engineers.

One of women inspired by Ulery was Aparna Singh, a doctoral candidate in applied physics at Caltech. The path to JPL is direct; it is managed by Caltech. One of 1,500 Caltech students working at JPL—but the only student who was a woman born outside the US—she followed Ulery's example by designing and developing algorithms to model NASA's Deep Space Network. When NASA launched Voyager 1, Singh was in the control room monitoring the automated, real-time tracking systems she developed.

LouAnn Epperson was the latest exotic talent at SMUG. Had she not completed two doctorates at MIT in only six years, the prodigy from the Rust Belt might have been working for a male industrial engineer at a Pittsburgh steel mill. In 1975, Irene Greif became the first woman to get a PhD in computer science from MIT. In 1976, LouAnn became the second.

At MIT, LouAnn conducted uncharted research in four unconventional labs: cognitive science, computer science, information science, and multimedia. Her dissertation established a research methodology to understand the convergence of technology, computing languages, media, and their impact on society. It was called Hopper's Quadrant after Grace Hopper, the Navy admiral who programmed the first generation of supercomputers and who popularized the idea of machine-independent programming languages.

When the nominally coeducational MIT struggled to find a faculty position or a progressive project for LouAnn, Caltech offered her a lab of her own to create a project of her choice. The offer owed more to the competitiveness between the rival technology institutions than it did to LouAnn's as yet undefined project.

* * *

"What is that odor?" Aparna Singh asked her colleague as they entered the recently sanitized lab in the basement of Booth. "Lysol?"

"No," Christina Duncan responded. "Testosterone."

Moments later, the whirlwind known as Adele Siegal provided SMUG with a quorum.

Siegal had traveled to Pasadena from Xerox's Palo Alto Research Center (PARC), where she was leading a project that made scant sense to the eggheads developing third-generation computers. With postgraduate degrees in information technology from the University of Michigan and in computing language from Carnegie Mellon, Siegal arrived at PARC with a mission to create an object-oriented language for computers that could be understood and used by human beings, not just mathematicians and geeks sequencing ones and zeros.

"Whoa. What's that perfume?" she asked, picking up the whiff of testosterone that had been discovered by her fellow researchers. "This has to be the nastiest lab I've ever been in."

"Had to be designed by one of those men in white shirts and skinny black ties," Siegal continued. "If they knew anything about design, they wouldn't dress the way they do."

Duncan and Singh nodded in mock agreement as they eyed the graphical interface designer and flamboyant drama queen with earth-goddess hair, wire-rimmed glasses, and flowered wrap dress.

Two hours after she disembarked at LAX, LouAnn Epperson joined her colleagues in the basement lab in Pasadena that had been assigned to her. Exhausted from lack of sleep and suffering from redeye jet lag, she would have to deal with awkward condolence sentiments from her colleagues. Then, she would ask them to plan their careers around her.

One by one, the members of SMUG approached their colleague and fellow survivor with sympathy.

"It must have been terrible," said Christina Duncan. Swaggering and stylish, the mechanical engineer from Virginia with the helmet of thick dark hair, piercing eyes, and a penchant for jeans, leather jackets, and scarves, gave LouAnn a curt hug that kept a respectable distance between bodies.

"It *was* terrible," LouAnn responded. "I was shown my father's body by a vampire then spent a week in shadows, darkness, and fear."

"Namaste."

Aparna Singh approached LouAnn with her hands pressed together in the gesture of *Pranamasana*, palms touching, fingers pointing upwards, and thumbs close to the chest. A striking woman with dark features and glowing teeth, she wore a colorful sari over a simple white blouse.

"I bow to the divine in you," she said softly, bending her mouth to LouAnn's ear where she whispered a Hindi prayer.

"That's lovely," LouAnn said. "What does it mean?"

"Never is the soul born, nor does it die at any time. It has never been brought into being, nor shall come hereafter—unborn, eternal, permanent, and ancient. When the body is slain, he is not slain."

"My father would appreciate the sentiments of time and life, Aparna, but I still struggle with them. But thank you."

Then LouAnn turned to embrace Adele Siegal.

"You know how the Jews are," Adela said, spreading her arms wide. "No afterlife. We sit shiva for a week, gorge ourselves on chopped liver, and argue endlessly about conducting industrious lives predetermined by our parents to get us into grad school." Laughter. Tears were neither expected, nor did they come. LouAnn gathered her friends in a group hug.

"Dear friends, this is all very touching," LouAnn said, maintaining the hug. "I love you dearly, but I admire you more. And I desperately need your help."

"How disappointing. I thought this was going to be a wake," Christina said. "I even brought the bourbon."

"Heavy drinking may be in order," LouAnn responded. "However, I can't afford to kill any of the brain cells in this room. I'll need them all for a very long time. Let me explain."

LouAnn described a sweeping project that involved technological determinism, the evolution of computer science, and the universal distribution of knowledge and intelligence to solve perplexing problems that impact society. She pledged to expose criminal activity by greedy corporations in collusion with the federal government. And she proposed to inform decisions that impact the way people work and live.

"We may even put a few despicable men in jail," she added.

The three other members of SMUG were silent for what seemed to be an eternity. Finally, Christina Duncan broke the silence.

"Is that all?" she asked. "What do you need from me? I like the part about putting despicable men in jail."

"I'm not sure exactly what I'm asking of you," LouAnn explained. "What I'm proposing is absolutely unreasonable and probably irrational. But it is scientific. Yet, in a strange way, I know I am doing the right thing by asking each of you to invest yourselves in my quest.

"Realistically, I'll need your help for twenty years or more. During that time, you'll be influencing organizations with vast resources and brainpower. You'll be running companies or labs, developing powerful new technologies, creating machines, and formulating policies for the private as well as the public sector, guiding government, and military policies, and—I say this with all due modesty—influencing changes in the world's social, economic, and political structure."

"Now you sound like my father," said Adele.

"I don't understand," said Aparna. "How will our careers—even as influential and powerful as you see them becoming—help your project? Which, if you don't mind me saying, sounds like a rehearsed, shallow answer that a beauty pageant contestant might give to a stupid question about a ridiculous notion of fostering world peace. It is an abstraction fraught with arrogance and ignorance, an equation of such complexity that the proposition alone can only be considered as an entertaining sound bite of the inane. No person, no group of people—not even women like us—can absorb the impossibly complex set of cultural and economic problems, or those fundamental to the natural laws and sciences of the planet, to solve problems on a global scale, even one molecule at a time. And your project is like that?"

"Exactly," said LouAnn.

"Well, then," said Christina, "count me in. I came prepared." She pulled a bottle of Jack Daniels and four shot glasses from her purse and then poured the bourbon into the glasses.

"Wait," said Aparna, who had already reconsidered LouAnn's proposal. "We must have peanuts."

With that, she pulled a bag of shelled peanuts from her sari. "There is a tradition at the Jet Propulsion Lab to eat good-luck peanuts before critical missions. Back in the sixties, the first successful Ranger mission to impact the moon occurred while a JPL staff member was eating peanuts. It became a good-luck charm."

"You carry peanuts with you?" Adele asked.

"You never know when you might have to change the world," said Aparna.

"Pass the bourbon and nuts," said Adele. "I'm in, too, now that drinking and snacks are involved."

Christina proposed the toast. "To LouAnn and her father. Who knows where they'll lead us? Time will tell."

The members of SMUG touched glasses, threw back the first of many shots of Jack Daniels, discarded peanut shells on the floor of a musty basement lab, and started to invent the future.

BABEL

As a researcher, LouAnn Epperson had come to terms with cognitive dissonance, the uncomfortable tension that comes with holding two conflicting thoughts in the mind at the same time. But as a daughter, she was conflicted about what she believed. Her father, Lou, was a pragmatist who believed that religion was an affront to logic and self-determination, an assault on free thought. Her mother, Ann, was a moralist who taught LouAnn to speak her mind, to have faith, and to find morality in the parables of the Bible. LouAnn took her name and purpose from both parents. From her father, she rejected divine intervention as a methodology for scientific outcomes. From her mother, she admired biblical metaphors for their wisdom and example. She currently fixated on the Tower of Babel story.

Everyone on Earth spoke the same language, the Babel story goes. Dispersed by the Great Flood, the people settled in the land of Shinar where they sought to make bricks and build a city with a tower that reached into the heavens. They pursued an ambition common to their ancestors far into the future: to make a name for themselves so that they would not be scattered over the world again.

In LouAnn's version, an insecure deity looked at the people's ambitions as a threat to divine power. God came down to look at the city and tower and observed that as one people with one language, nothing that they sought would be out of their reach. In the biblical version, Genesis 11:4–9, the story goes like this:

> Come, let us go down and there confuse their
> language, that they may not understand one
> another's speech. So the Lord scattered them
> abroad from there over the face of all the earth,
> and they ceased building the city.

To LouAnn, the Bible's "Lord" sounded a lot like the men running Caltech. Justifying a project that would enable ordinary people to tap into knowledge closely held by the powerful was improbable at best. The men at Caltech already considered themselves deity. They were not about to let a brash mortal, a too-young woman from Smokestack, Ohio, mess with their kingdom of heaven.

Even if LouAnn could somehow persuade the celestial dictators at Caltech that pervasive computing could help solve some of the world's most pressing problems, she would have to navigate her way through scientific Babel. Computers were evolving from wartime calculation machines such as the Turing machine, the British Colossus, and the American ENIAC—mechanical beasts that filled rooms with levers, switches, and cables. These machines were being replaced with distributed computing from desktop machines for the office, the classroom, and the home, each programmed for a multitude of different tasks.

In computing, source code is written using a human-readable computer language that sends instructions to a machine. It can enable a simple specific task or solve the complex algorithms of scientific equations. Like Babel, the world of computers was a jumble of code that could only be understood by one model of one machine or one program designed for a specific task.

At Caltech's Jet Propulsion Lab, America's early aerospace engineers ignored computers because they considered programming as women's work. But it took women to figure it out. Ironically, Caltech became a pioneer in hiring women to program computers.

Sexism held back space exploration by a decade, LouAnn calculated. In 1979, it was delaying discoveries and advances in virtually every field. LouAnn earned doctorates in technology and computer science in a shorter time than any man in history. But her peers at the two most prestigious technology institutions in the US still dismissed female computer scientists as clerical workers. What a waste of time.

At the nation's top research universities, scientific inquiry was divided into two categories: science that had already been done and science that probably wouldn't be done. Caltech was content with its Jet Propulsion Lab that sent spacecraft into the solar system. The institute also remained overly admiring of its celebrity physicists like Richard Perriman and frequent guest lecturer Stephen Hawking, both of whom postulated about a theoretical universe. Science and academia had lost faith in the idea that there was anything truly big or exciting left to be discovered in the physical world.

It wasn't always that way. Before the Earth was fully mapped, explorers made discoveries all the time. Now exploration was limited by the assumption that everything important and achievable had been discovered. Her peers had it wrong, LouAnn insisted. There were universal mysteries to be solved—the discoverable secret code, she called it. You just have to know where and how to look.

It's was freeing to think that breakthrough ideas were out there, waiting to be discovered, rather than to be argued in the mind. While the favored approach in the seventies was to shake up an existing institution, LouAnn understood that such disruption would inevitably cause her to think in institutional terms, to become stuck in old practices.

She told herself that the basic challenge was to find things that were hard to prove but could be proved. *Find a frontier without accepting others' definitions of the frontier*, she told herself. Whether you're trying to make sense of the universe or organize all the world's information, you can't fall into the trap of assuming that if an idea were any good, someone would already have had it. That's how everyone else thinks.

Fortunately, many Caltech students thought like LouAnn. Like her, they were junior geniuses in math, engineering, the applied sciences, physics, and the humanities, searching for a breakthrough that would define their lives. LouAnn presented them with a set of problems that, if solved, would usher in an era of intelligence and discovery. They related immediately to the young computer scientist from MIT just a few years older than they were. They flocked to the strange lab in the basement of Booth Hall with the cool new computers that fit on a table.

Caltech students were also noted for their irreverence. Pranks were a tradition. Many aimed at their rivals at MIT. But rookie pranksters honed their skills with intracampus mischief and rivalries. One such rivalry played out during the final week of classes in 1977.

* * *

It was *Star Trek* Night in the basement of Booth Hall. Students packed the room. The popular show, now in reruns, was a favorite of Caltrekkies who held silly-serious debates over the future technology and inexplicable science that propelled the Starship Enterprise through deep space at warp speed. Rival groups had formed. One was the computer science majors who studied with LouAnn. The other was the physics wonks who worshipped at the feats of Richard Perriman, Caltech's famous Nobel laureate. LouAnn's crew staged a mock, late-night TV talk show to clear minds with humor just before the tension of finals week.

The familiar *Star Trek* theme, playing from a tape recorder wired to speakers, announced the start of the show. Then Captain James T. Kirk appeared in a Starfleet uniform, or at least a quasi-familiar version of one.

"Welcome to Boldly Go, the show exploring the universe's biggest mysteries," the Kirk character said. "Tonight, we go where no discriminating being has gone before: Pasadena, California. Our guest: Nobel Prize-winning physics professor, raconteur, and big man on campus, the Big Dick himself, Richard P. Perriman. And now your host, Mr. Spock."

Spock, in full Vulcan guise with pointed ears, arched eyebrows, and slicked-down hair, came to the fore and gave the Vulcan salute to enthusiastic applause.

"The Vulcan monologue," he explained. "Not funny but logical."

Spock sat behind a desk as Kirk took a seat at the adjacent couch.

"Great audience tonight, Mr. Spock—Romulans, Martians, and a few horny humanoids from a small colony known as Caltech," Kirk said in talk-show banter. Laughter.

"We shall keep things simple, then, Jim. Our first guest needs no introduction in these coordinates. He's a physicist and author, a Nobel Prize winner who helped develop a minor weapon of mass destruction called the atomic bomb. Please welcome Professor Richard Perriman."

A Perriman doppelgänger walked from the audience and sat between Spock and Kirk.

Spock started the interview with a curiosity: "What keeps a scientific explorer such as yourself in this insignificant part of the universe?"

"It's the fame and the sex," the Perriman doppelganger answered, bringing hearty laughter from the audience.

"Our computers confirm your hypothesis, Professor Perriman. There's the woman from Brazil you brought to Pasadena, the cheerleaders at UCLA, and, apparently, some bimbos from a place called Las Vegas. As a fellow science officer, could you explain the meaning of the term *bimbo*?" More laughter.

"It means life is good for a Nobel Prize winner," said the smiling Perriman character.

"As you know, television has made me something of a sex symbol myself," Spock boasted. "Take a look at this." He raised one eyebrow and flashed the suave Vulcan look.

Eyebrow raised, the Perriman character struck the same pose.

"Now we shall mind meld," said Spock as the two leaned toward one another, joining foreheads.

"Oh, baby," cooed the Perriman character.

"Better than Earth sex," said Spock, flashing the Vulcan salute to the audience. "Live long and prosper."

* * *

Amid laughter and applause, LouAnn Epperson answered the phone in the basement lab that had become a burlesque stage. Her amusement with the *Star Trek* skit changed as she listened to the call.

"What was that about?" asked Christina Duncan, who was standing next to LouAnn.

"SMUG alert," she said. "That was Janet in the provost's office. A special committee is going to reconsider my funding. They've called a hearing for 7:30 a.m. on Monday. I'm so screwed."

Duncan tried to talk her off the ledge. "We'll make the case at a hearing. Do you know who's on the committee?"

"That's the problem," LouAnn explained. "Provost Stempler, of course. Mattuck in Math. Stokes in Engineering and Applied Sciences."

"Not good," Duncan said. "They're relics."

"That's not the worst of it," LouAnn continued. "Perriman. He came to deliver the hearing notification to me personally. He's here now."

Of all the times Richard Perriman could have visited my lab, he chooses the moment my students are poking fun at him. Quantum physics arrives with ironic timing.

As if on cue, the real Richard P. Perriman walked from the audience to join his doppelgänger and Mr. Spock in the Vulcan salute. The students roared.

LouAnn looked at the two Perrimans and the student dressed as Spock.

"Did you know the Spock character is inspirational to many serious scientists," she said to Christina. "Leonard Nimoy, the actor who plays Spock, has said that, on meeting him, scientists were eager to show him their work and discuss it with him as if he were a peer. Nimoy is an accomplished actor, photographer, and poet. His response to scientists in those situations was this: 'It certainly looks like you're headed in the right direction.'"

"It certainly looks like you're headed in the right direction," Christina joked, trying to comfort her friend.

> Come, let us go down and there confuse their language, that they may not understand one another's speech. So the Lord scattered them abroad from there over the face of all the earth, and they ceased building the city.

RIDE OF THE VALKYRIES

At precisely 7:00 a.m., "Ride of the Valkyries" blared from every loudspeaker on the Caltech campus. As the music rose to crescendo at an earsplitting volume, underclassmen emerged from all-night study sessions, heavily caffeinated or buzzed on uppers. They moved across campus, messy-haired and mostly without shoes, their shoulders hunched against the early morning chill in a choreographed tradition known as finals week.

LouAnn Epperson was already heading across the campus to her final exam. With a grudging knowledge of German opera forced upon her by her mother, she immediately recognized the irony: the beginning of act three of Wagner's ridiculous "*Die Walküre*." The curtain rises to reveal a mountain peak where four of the eight Valkyrie sisters of Brünnhilde gather in preparation for the transportation of fallen heroes to Valhalla. As they are joined by the other four, the "Ride of the Valkyries" is carried by the orchestra as the Valkyries greet each other and sing their battle cry.

Why not? I could use a good battle cry.

She walked through a grove of olive eucalyptus trees and then past a sign that said "Members Only," entering Caltech's ornate faculty club, the Athenaeum, to the final notes of "The Valkyries."

Built to impress, "the Ath," as insiders called it, had the look of an overdone Italian villa with buff-colored masonry walls, a red-tile roof, and Andalusian-style wrought iron over huge arched windows. Alternately sophisticated and quirky, intimate and imposing, the Ath was as contradictory as Caltech itself.

As she moved inside, LouAnn was approached by a well-groomed man in a crisp business suit. A silver name badge on his breast pocket displayed the name by which he was known in the Ath: Manuel Monterrey.

"Call me Manny," said the Athenaeum's greeter and unofficial tour guide. "And it's Martinez, not Monterrey. Monterey is where I'm from. Why that's important, I'm not sure. It's a Pasadena thing."

"Pleased to meet you, Manny. I'm LouAnn from Youngstown, Ohio. Fortunately, no one calls me LouAnn Youngtown, but I've only been in Pasadena a few months."

"Would it be alright if I called you Professor Epperson?" Manny asked.

"That would be my pleasure…" LouAnn responded, "assuming I'll be invited back to this place."

As they began a slow walk inside the Ath, the Mexican concierge who couldn't use his last name at the faculty club began to explain the arcane rules to a faculty member who couldn't join because she was a woman: No money changes hands. Guest fees must be covered by a member. Members order by filling out chits and handing them to Jason Chemistry or Alex Engineering, well-scrubbed student waiters wearing uniforms and badges such as Manny's that declared both their name and their major.

Manny led LouAnn through a clubby world of pillars and arches, spaces and angles lit by a rooftop skylight. They passed rooms decorated in burnished oak and black walnut with heavy antique furniture. When they reached a winding marble staircase that opened to three floors, Manny paused.

"I'm sure you've heard the stories about Albert Einstein living upstairs in the faculty residences for a time," he said, looking up the stairway to heaven.

LouAnn instantly grasped the physics of the moment: "Just a guess, Manny, but I don't think we're headed in that direction."

"Actually, we'll be going downstairs."

"It's all relative," LouAnn said.

If Manny caught the joke, he was not inclined to throw it back.

"Obscure Einstein joke," LouAnn apologized.

Looking like he wanted to flee the smart-mouthed professor, Manny took to the stairs and headed down. LouAnn followed him to the ornate Hayman Lounge, where the greeter-guide acknowledged the photographic pantheon of Caltech Nobel laureates, all looking constipated, peering down from the walls.

Recovering from her humor foul, LouAnn added an obvious but overlooked fact to the greeter's repertoire.

"Manny, are you aware that the Athenaeum derives its name from Athena, the Greek goddess of wisdom?"

"No, professor, I was not. But I shall remember the reference," he said. "It seems that men always fill this room. They seem to be here now."

Indeed they were. The five members of the Administrative Committee on Sponsored Research had arrived an hour earlier. They lingered presently over a hearty California breakfast buffet that included mimosas, fruit juices, huevos rancheros, eggs benedict, chorizo, bacon, poached salmon, Lyonnaise potatoes, assorted garnishments, bagels, muffins, granola, yogurt, and enough California fruit to make the San Joaquin Valley look barren.

"We'll be with you in a moment, Professor Epperson," said Edward Stempler, Caltech's provost and the chair of the committee. "I'm sure Manny can find you a cup of coffee."

I'd kill for a coffee. Might even be able to pour one myself.

Caffeine was required, so LouAnn chose not to dignify Stempler's indifference.

You didn't have to invite me to eat at the trough, Stempler, but you could have acknowledged me with a bit of collegial courtesy.

LouAnn nodded politely as Manny made the coffee run.

"Don't let the big swinging dicks intimidate you," came a voice from behind her.

"Christina?"

"Thought I'd lend a little moral support," said Christina Duncan. "I brought a friend. Meet Noah Altman."

"Pleasure, Professor," Altman said. "Perhaps we'll have time to talk later."

With that, he turned and walked toward the large rectangular conference table where the big swinging dicks were taking their seats. LouAnn could only turn her palms skyward and mouth a question to Christina—*who was that?*—before Stempler called the meeting to order.

"We'll be expeditious," she heard Stempler say. The provost was not prone to wasting time over a foregone conclusion.

As the operatic sound track announcing finals week ended, LouAnn Epperson readied for her oral exam. She really needed that cup of coffee.

* * *

The circumspect Stempler began the hearing expressing his authority and taking control: "For those of you who may not know me— that would only be you, Professor Epperson—I am the provost of the California Institute of Technology. I chair the Administrative Committee on Sponsored Research.

"At Caltech, we consider research a privileged endeavor. In 1923, Robert Millikan, who had just won the Nobel Prize for physics, formulated the Institute's distinguished research agenda that we consider here today. His colleague, Albert Einstein, completed the theory of relativity here as part of that agenda. More recently, Linus Pauling was bestowed the Nobel Prize for Chemistry as a faculty member and the Nobel Peace Prize as research fellow at the Institute. Professor Perriman, who serves on the faculty as well as this committee, received the Nobel Prize for Physics for his development of quantum electrodynamics.

"We are here today to live up to their examples. The Administrative Committee on Sponsored Research considers projects that the Institute undertakes—frequently with the support of sponsors—that fulfill the expectations of the men whose photographs hang in this room.

"The purpose of this hearing is quite simple: to determine whether the Institute will sponsor, or facilitate in some manner, a project or theory under the direction of a distinguished researcher. To that end, we are convening a panel of distinguished academic investigators, as well as prominent stakeholders, representing the Institute and its interests.

"Each has considered this case. Since some circumstances are unusual, the applicant—ah, I suppose that is the word for you, Professor Epperson—may not be fully acquainted with members of the committee. I shall introduce them before their questions, should they have any.

"Professor Epperson, you will be granted time to make a statement about your project. You will be asked to defend your research, your hypotheses, your outcomes, and your expectations.

"Are there questions about this process?

Stempler led her to the trap that had been set at breakfast.

"One question, Provost Stempler," came the expected response from the founder and director of the little-known NexUs Lab. "I was informed of this hearing just a few days ago. Is it the policy of the Institute to secretly investigate a research initiative over a period of weeks then determine its future without timely notification and due process, denying its director reasonable time for academic defense?"

The first of the big swinging dicks was lying in wait. Richard K. Stokes, dean of the School of Engineering and Applied Sciences moved in for the kill:

"It's a test, dear girl. Certainly the rigor of education at MIT prepared you for academic inquiry. We assume a female colleague can think on her feet. After all, you earned a PhD. Are the orals in Cambridge so lacking the academic rigor of Socratic discourse that doctoral candidates can't demonstrate their competency in extemporaneous critical thinking?"

What the fuck? They think girls can't play. You want to play? Then pull up your zippers.

"I beg your indulgence, Dean Stokes. You are correct: I'm just a dear girl who somehow managed to talk her way to a master's degree and *two* doctorates at MIT in six years—a feat that exhibits some small measure of academic achievement and critical thinking. No doubt, the esteemed scholars at Caltech will rationalize such apparent competency to declining academic rigor at an East Coast technical college masquerading as a world-class technology institute.

"My credentials may be tarnished here by my choice of technological institutes, gentlemen, but my MIT education has left me intellectually curious about why I was recruited so aggressively by Caltech. Just another prank to prove superiority over a rival to please the gods who gather here this morning in the Athenaeum? If that scenario was not so cynical, so utterly insulting, so cloyingly sexist, so beneath the integrity of this institute, I would find it amusing."

The first dick was left holding this.

The second dick was thoroughly aroused. "Bravo, Professor," chortled Richard Perriman.

Stempler was having none of it. He rose to defend his dean who brought $120 million annually to Caltech in donations, endowments, sponsorships, equipment, research grants, consulting, and speaking fees. At a university where tuition covered less than half of instruction costs, the principal role of the dean was to raise money. And Stokes was very good at it.

"I don't know how the protocol works at MIT, Professor Epperson, but deans at Caltech earn respect. Dean Stokes warrants ours. I should remind you that it is not in your interests as a Caltech professor to alienate colleagues. Let's keep that in mind as we move on, shall we?"

LouAnn took the point grudgingly as Stempler shot her a look indicating that she had lost round one.

* * *

Round two. The provost proceeded with an agenda intended to expedite the obvious: a statement and questions from Arthur Mattuck, the prosaic dean of the mathematics school and landlord of LouAnn's lab in the basement of Booth Hall.

Mattuck: Provost Stempler, distinguished colleagues. I am unable to make a meaningful statement about Professor Epperson's project beyond what is already unknown. Even as the dean who hosts her computer lab in the basement of Booth, I know little about what is going on in the basement. So, yes, I have a few pertinent questions: Professor, have you ever attended a faculty meeting of the mathematics department?

LouAnn: I wasn't aware I was on the faculty of the mathematics department.

Mattuck: Nor am I. Do you have an explanation?

LouAnn: One comes to mind, Dean Mattuck. Caltech didn't admit women undergraduates until 1970. That was only seven years ago. Four women received bachelor's degrees at the Institute in 1973, none in mathematics. That was only four years ago. The Institute has yet to award a doctorate in mathematics to a woman. Since it requires about six years to earn a doctorate, and several more years to achieve the required teaching or research experience, it is reasonable to conclude that in 1977, that a woman would not serve on the mathematics faculty unless the department recruited one from another institution. Is my math correct, Dean Mattuck?

Mattuck: You get an A, Professor Epperson. Or would you prefer the popular honorific *miss*?

"That's enough, Arthur," came an unexpected admonishment from Stempler. "The principle of respect at this institute will be applied equally among colleagues of both genders."

"No, it is not enough, Edward," Mattuck shot back. "We cannot let a moment of gender politics impact the critical calculations that men of science have traditionally advanced at this institute. Would you admit women just to distract my mathematicians and to marry them off?"

"I said that's enough, Arthur." Having defended one dean for arrogance that was earned, Stempler was obliged to call out another for sexism that was institutionalized.

Caltech had been a bastion of sexism since its founding as a vocational school in 1891. Its reputation as a brainy boy's club gained momentum throughout the twentieth century until the feminist movement of the 1970s fought for equal rights in education and business. The Institute's admission and hiring practices came under scrutiny in the decade as Caltech lost talented students, teachers, and endowments to competing universities such as Stanford and the University of California at Berkeley.

"This line of questioning is not helpful," Stempler said again. "The Institute began a program in 1970 to address a blemish that has impacted the Institute's advancement. Let's move along. I believe it is time to hear from Professor Epperson about her laboratory."

Round two to one of the few women at Caltech who weren't working as assistants, secretaries, or human computers. Stempler called a short break to prepare for LouAnn Epperson, the bitchy, brilliant researcher with a mission.

THE GHOST IN THE ATH

As the opera in the Hayman Lounge of the Athenaeum reached intermission, the players moved in multiple directions around the stage, some grazing at the replenished buffet, some refilling their cups at the coffee urn, and some sprinting to the bathrooms.

The activity was dizzying. Exhausted from lack of sleep, relentless rehearsals, and academic jousting, LouAnn sat mesmerized, watching the room become a blur. A shadowy figure came into focus near the portraits hanging on the wall. He was wearing a yellow hard hat, white short-sleeved shirt, work boots, and Dickies work pants that pulled a ring of keys hanging from his belt.

He carried a metal lunch pail.

Daddy?

The apparition was preoccupied with the portraits and the creature comforts of the room:

"Lots of smart people in this room," the Timekeeper observed. "Nobel Prize winners, huh? So why do all these smart guys look so miserable. You get a couple hundred grand if you win that prize, don't you? Serious money. What's there to be angry about? I mean, look at the spread on that buffet. California sure knows how to grow produce. Do you think they'd mind if I poached some fruit? I brought my own coffee."

The apparition opened his lunch pail, removed a thermos, and placed it next to the fruit on the buffet table. He put an orange in the lunch pail then moved to the grapes. Popping one in his mouth, he turned his stream-of-consciousness banter toward LouAnn.

"You do realize, my brilliant daughter, that you can't beat them. So you might want to explain what's in it for them. Wash it down with a cup of humility. Must go. I want to check out the rest of this joint before I head off to work. Word is that Einstein lived upstairs while finishing his theory of relativity. Relativity. Good concept."

The apparition picked up his lunch pail and disappeared into the bright light of the stairway.

ATHENA SMILES

"You have made Athena smile, LouAnn."

Richard Perriman was characteristically complementary, but he was not about to let a young and untested researcher—a woman—steal his status as Caltech's favored genius-god. Not in *the* Athenaeum. Not in his universe. So the renowned physicist invoked his expertise: intellectual intimidation.

"Newtonian physics claimed that things have an objective reality separate from our perception of them," he began. "Quantum physics introduces uncertainty. It reveals that as the perception of an object changes, the object itself literally changes. So I wonder, LouAnn, whether your reality is the objective reality or simply your perception of it?"

Quantum physics? Leave it to Perriman to bully me with theoretical science. And what's this LouAnn stuff? Suddenly, I'm no longer Professor Epperson?

"Then do let me express my perception, *Richard*," LouAnn shot back to the Nobel Prize winner. "According to your boy Stephen Hawking, humanity's deepest desire for knowledge is justification enough for our continuing quest. Unlike the quantum physicist, the computer scientist can validate theory with an abundance of verifiable data. Our goal is nothing less than a complete accounting of the universe in which we live. We can do that with the data from pervasive computing."

In LouAnn's argument, Perriman saw vulnerability: her unwavering self-confidence.

"Accomplished scientists are accustomed to the disappointment of failed experiments in the lab or equations that fail to prove the desired result," he lectured. "The learnings they take from endless failures, anomalies, or unexpected behaviors are considered even more valuable than the breakthrough moments of invention or leaps in knowledge or understanding. Researchers must be conditioned to handle any circumstance, any outcome, any obstacle. Even gender discrimination.

"You are afflicted with scientific ego, Professor. You lack the experience, the character, and the humility to execute an overly ambitious experiment. Do you even have a methodology that presents a demonstrable path to desired results?"

Thank you for asking, you brilliant bastard.

LouAnn reached into her tote and pulled out a Rubik's Cube.

"Here's our methodology. You may recognize it as a toy, a 3-D combination puzzle invented two years ago by a Hungarian sculptor and professor of architecture."

As she talked, LouAnn began twisting color-coded components on the cube. "There are six sides, each with nine moveable components," she explained. "One of six colors is assigned to each component. The idea is to work the components to get one color on each of the six sides.

"At the NexUs lab, we use the cube as an investigative model, a research metaphor. Each face represents a common area of investigation or inquiry. The color-coded components are subsets for action or discovery. When we solve the puzzle with all its combinations, we reset and play again."

Perriman was fascinated. "Want to give a go, Professor?" LouAnn asked. "So far I've managed to get a few yellow squares on one side of the cube for you."

Perriman took the cube and considered it studiously. He twisted and turned it until one side came up entirely yellow. Then he returned it to LouAnn feeling proud of himself.

"Congratulations, Professor. You just completed several thousand calculations just to arrange one face of the cube in one color.

I'll have one of our undergraduate computer operators send you the equation that you just solved.

"But here's the real challenge," LouAnn explained, taking back the cube, turning and twisting the components in three directions as she talked. "There are five sides to go. To complete the second side, you have to move some of the yellow squares on the completed side to get to the right combination of colors. Same thing with the other four sides. With each side, the permutations become increasingly problematic. You have to continually disrupt your successes to reach a solution."

LouAnn continued to twist and turn the components as she talked: "From our data, we have concluded that Rubik's Cube has three billion combinations but only one solution. The human brain is a powerful processor. Any Caltech freshman scan solve Rubik's Cube in about one hundred moves or in about ten minutes or less. It takes a properly programmed IBM 5100 computer about three seconds to solve the puzzle. I'm a little slower."

With that, LouAnn set the cube on the conference table. The puzzle was solved, each face of the cube displaying one color. "Just a little trick I learned at MIT."

"How long did it take you to rehearse that?" asked Perriman, shaking his head.

"Pretty much all weekend," LouAnn confessed.

* * *

Stempler had grown impatient with the tedious, academic one-up-manship that he considered irrelevant. He decided that the foregone conclusion had been tortured long enough.

"It is time to consider whether the lab called NexUs will continue as part of the Institute's research mission," he announced. "While the recommendation to the president and the board of trustees is mine, I shall be guided by the wisdom of this committee. It's time to vote. As the host school, we'll start with you, Dean Mattuck. Then Dean Stokes and Professor Perriman."

Mattuck: Ms. Epperson's imagination is vivid. Her tricks are entertaining, but her theories are pure conjecture. Mathematicians resolve the truth or falsity of conjecture with mathematical proof. That is what we do here at Caltech. Should this institute support a frivolous agenda that mocks our traditions? Not in my house. I vote no.

Stokes: I just don't see it. Sorry, Professor.

Perriman: Yes for me, but with qualification. Mathematics doesn't want it. Engineering and Applied Sciences can't understand it. Physics will take it.

"And who would direct it?" LouAnn asked.

"You would, LouAnn. But under my guidance, of course."

LouAnn saw where this was going. "Then I vote no on behalf of Professor Perriman," she injected.

Stempler was now shaking his head, ready to put an end to the joust. "I, too, am persuaded to vote against the continuation of the NexUs lab. With neither a host department nor a sponsor to pay for the activities of the lab, the Institute is put in a untenable position. An obligation to fund an open-ended project of dubious value is simply unacceptable. We are looking down a rabbit hole."

LouAnn sank in her chair as Stempler moved to nail the coffin shut. But one witness had not been heard: Noah Altman.

Altman was an accomplished yet little-known innovator. As an electrical engineer at RCA, he invented the technology for liquid crystal displays (LCDs). But in 1975, he quietly left RCA to join the Defense Department as head of the Defense Advanced Research Projects Agency. Altman managed influential connections between Caltech and the Defense Department as special assistant to the secretary of defense, performing long-range research and development planning. When Harold Brown resigned as president of Caltech to become secretary of defense under Jimmy Carter, Brown was succeeded at Caltech by physicist Robert Christy, who worked with Perriman on the Manhattan Project that produced the atomic bomb. As interim president, the physicist Christy had no interest in lesser projects. He called on Altman to disarm a young professor—a woman from MIT, no less—at an academic hearing on whether Caltech should fund something called an advanced computing lab.

Cautious about his relationship with the new president of Caltech and cognizant of Altman's influence, Provost Stempler astutely deferred to the guest from Washington:

"At this time, I'd like to recognize Mr. Altman, who was invited to attend these proceedings by President Christy and members of the board of trustees."

"Thank you, Provost Stempler," said Altman, speaking his first words since the hearing began. "I came to Pasadena following briefings I conducted with experts in Palo Alto and in the California corridor that some are now calling 'the Silicon Valley.' One of the experts with whom I consulted was Professor Donald Knauff. As you may know, Professor Knauff is a Caltech alumni who currently serves on the faculty at Stanford and was recently named to the National Academy of Sciences. He is the author of *The Language of Computers* and is an esteemed scientist who advises the Institute for Defense Analysis. He asked me to deliver this letter to the committee. I think it should be considered now."

Altman handed the sealed letter to Stempler, who opened it and read out loud:

> LouAnn Epperson is onto something. Cut the Caltech crap and give her what she needs. Otherwise Stanford will hire her.
>
> Don Knauff

Perriman chuckled as Mattuck and Stokes groaned in unison.

"Clearly, we have dissonance on this matter," Altman intervened. "Perhaps I can help bring the problem to a resolution. At the agency I direct, I have developed a set of questions to evaluate proposed research programs. The questions have come to be known in scientific circles as the Altman Catechism. They are quite simple:

"What are you trying to do? Articulate your objectives using absolutely no jargon.

"How is it done today, and what are the limits of current practice?

"What's new in your approach, and why do you think it will be successful?

"Who cares? If you're successful, what difference will it make? What are the risks and the payoffs?

"How much will it cost? How long will it take? What are the exams to check for success?

"With the exception of the last set of questions, Professor Epperson has provided answers worthy of our support, our admiration, and our imagination. As for funding and the length of the project, my colleagues in Washington can handle those, so let's remove them as obstacles."

Altman then asked to speak privately with Stempler. The two moved to a corner of the room, conferred briefly, then returned to the conference table.

"Mr. Altman has steered us through the awkward moment," Stempler explained. "I've just been informed that the Institute now has a generous sponsor for the research lab known as NexUs. Professor Epperson, you'll have what you need at Caltech for as long as you need it. Congratulations."

What just happened?

Stunned, smart-mouthed LouAnn Epperson was speechless for the first time that anyone could remember.

Across the room, Manny Monterrey returned to the Hayman Lounge to see the committee out of the Ath. He caught the eye of the provost, who looked as if the weight of the gods had been lifted from his shoulders.

"Manny," Stempler called, "we'll need an application for Professor Epperson. I believe she is about to become the first woman member of the Athenaeum."

LouAnn and Christina embraced, but the women did not allow themselves to celebrate excessively, or in any way that might be construed as overtly female. Their shrieking, jumping-up-and-down dance would come later, after they left the Ath.

"I still don't get it," LouAnn asked her new best friend. "What's with this Altman character?"

"It's complicated," Duncan tried to explain. "Don't let it get around, but I work for him. We're playing with the big boys, sister."

"And Knauff?"

"That was Adele's handiwork," Christina explained. "Knauff owes her. Couldn't have written his book without her."

Perriman soon found them. "Quite a show, ladies," he said, mustering all his charm. "Who needs Vegas when you have Caltech? See you around campus."

On his way to fetch an application for the faculty club, Manny paused at the buffet table where the impressive platter of fruit remained half-consumed. He was ready to instruct the kitchen crew to remove the platter when he spotted a container that didn't belong.

"Did anyone leave this behind?" he asked, holding up a thermos made to fit inside an industrial lunch box.

"My father did," said the Timekeeper's daughter.

PART FIVE

THE FAMILIAR STRANGER

THE FAMILIAR STRANGER

Separated by their destinies, LouAnn Epperson and Jordan Maier lived their lives apart. Gradually, without even noticing it, they found their fate in the distant days of familiar circumstances.

Three months after Black Monday, an internal staff report from the Antitrust Division of the US Department of Justice recommended that the government reject the proposed merger of Sykes Corp. and Jones & Laughline Steel. The report refuted claims from the companies that Youngstown Steel was a failing company. It concluded that plant closings in Youngstown were conducted to justify an anticompetitive merger intended to consolidate the nation's steel and shipping industries.

One year after the closing of Youngstown Steel's Campbell Works, US Attorney General Winston Dell approved the Sykes-LTV merger, disregarding the investigation by the Antitrust Division that determined the merger was illegal. The Youngstown Steel name and all company records disappeared.

Subsequently, the Carter administration refused to fund reopening steel mills in Youngstown under community-worker ownership. It also withdrew $350 million pledged for projects to revitalize Youngstown, a vital cog in the nation's industrial legacy.

Jennings Landry, the president of Youngstown Steel, was transferred to dismantle what was left of the American steel industry. Ostracized in his hometown of New Orleans, he was exiled to Pittsburgh. There, he committed suicide when he was diagnosed with steelworkers' disease: pancreatic cancer.

Landon Daumbrelle, Landry's son-in-law who served as Youngstown Steel's vice president, returned to his hometown of New Orleans where he became chief marketing officer of the Sykes family's shipping and agribusiness empire.

Jordan Maier remained in Youngstown to chronicle the decline of the steel industry and the demise of his hometown.

LouAnn Epperson worked anonymously on special assignments for the Defense Advanced Research Projects Agency. She secretly returned to Youngstown to make amends.

THE SLAG HEAP

In the dramatic climax of steelmaking, iron is blasted into molten steel inside a towering furnace. At 1,500 degrees, it flows into a giant ladle, which transports the fiery goo to molds where it is poured to form ingots. The series of chemical reactions leaves fused deposits that are drawn off the blast furnace. The deposits, known as slag, are stacked in heaps outside the mills.

Youngstown devolved into a slag heap. In the decades that followed Black Monday, the city lost tens of thousands of jobs, half of its population, and entire neighborhoods to urban decay. One by one, the hulking mills that hugged the Mahoning River came down, the towering blast furnaces toppled in demolitions that spread dust, fumes, and rubble across seventeen miles of wasteland along the still-toxic river.

As Youngstown entered the twenty-first century, more than one-third of remaining residents lived below the poverty line. Nearly 20 percent were unemployed. While crime and corruption had always been part of the Youngstown's dark side, bad deeds escalated as resources for public safety were depleted. The unemployed routinely set fire to houses they could not maintain. Crack houses operated in the houses that stood. Residents with jobs and money fled to the suburbs south of the city, while an underclass for the hopeless emerged in apocalyptic obsolescence. A congressman, sheriff, prosecutor, county commissioner, and several judges were indicted and imprisoned in the nefarious political system that passed for civic leadership,

A rough city became a harsh one. A street author described Youngstown this way in the Urban Dictionary: "Where Satan threatens to send residents of hell who are deemed unworthy...This desolate, barren wasteland was at one time an important manufacturer of steel..."

The description came with a warning: "Mess with Youngstown (the fucking Valley to you) and you will get skinned alive if you are lucky."

* * *

Jordan Mailer sorted through the slag heap for stories the way prisoners at concentration camps scavenged bodies for gold fillings: he approached the job with shame, contempt, and a will to survive. He had intended to leave Youngstown for a place that was more palatable and to work at an influential newspaper more worthy of his talent. Newspapers, however, were mired in their own decline. As with steel mills, newspapers closed as readers turned to the Internet for ubiquitous access to news. Staffing and salaries cratered across the industry.

Destiny crushed Jordan by refusing his wishes and by fulfilling them. He was brought to a time and place to chronicle a moment of consequential change. Fate delivered him to the slag heap. He took the metaphor personally. While he admired steelworkers for pursuing a limited existence in Youngstown, Jordan questioned their choices. Presented with the certainty of failure, they became foregone conclusions, accepting their fates as victims of an inevitable outcome, trading temporary security for a promise they knew would never be fulfilled. They lived the hard way. And they knew it.

So did Jordan. There were more attractive paths to fulfillment than working as a reporter at *The Youngstown Examiner*. The years brought a strange commitment to his hometown with recurring doubt about his job. Did he lack the talent to escape? Or the will? The complicated questions tormented him.

Part of human nature allows us to control the other part of human nature. Even though humans tend to be unreasonable, it isn't because they are incapable of reason. Even if we backslide to irrationality, we should indulge hope when deliberating how to run our lives.

"Death of the Timekeeper" was the most important, arguably the best, story Jordan Maier would ever write. It was written when he was a novice journalist. The stories that followed should have been more important, the unresolved issues more probing, and the reporting even more meaningful. Jordan's stories were serviceable yet somehow insufficient. The fatalism with which he wrote could not be edited out. He felt as if he was letting down Youngstown, letting down himself, and letting down LouAnn. She was the brilliant one, and she was long gone. As with slag, only despair remained.

TIME CATCHES UP

Present time

Tampa was the perfect place for a hoodlum to blend. It was Youngstown with sunshine instead of smoke. From Ybor City, Tampa's historic tourist trap, mobsters from the Traficante, Longo, Genovese, Gambino, Lucchese, and Bonanno families ran bootleg rum, Cuban cigars, prostitution rings, and bolita—the Florida version of the gambling lottery known in the Northeast as "The Bug." Operating under the protection of the mob families, small-time gangsters from northern cities were sent to the Big Guava to round up the easy money from the game that was popular among working class Cubans, Hispanics, Italians, and blacks. C. J. Russo was one of the gangsters-in-residence.

Russo had skills that kept him useful, which was to say, alive. The former security chief at Youngstown Steel was assigned to Sunshine Downs, the thoroughbred racetrack that was run by organized crime to launder the profits from bolita and other illegal activities. His job was to keep the losers away from the goodfellas at the track and to ensure that the daily fix was in. Money flowed from illegal activities, only to be legitimized in legal bets placed at the track.

After the day's races were won by all the right horses, after the money was counted and delivered, Russo—an enforcer and a bag man—returned routinely to his musty, Florida-style cottage in Oldsmar just a few blocks from Sunshine Downs and Old Tampa Bay. There, he lived a solitary existence, medicated by rum and

Cokes, where he watched *deportes* and telenovelas on Univision until he fell asleep.

On this day, Russo sat alone in one of the open-air boxes of trackside seats, content in his solitude during the lull between races, his face buried in the *Daily Racing Form*. His peace was interrupted by a man wearing a panama hat and sunglasses. A loose-fitting flowered shirt was draped over muscle, and a Glock 21 stuffed in his pants.

"You mind?" asked the muscle in the panama.

Russo had learned to avoid trouble. He hid his face behind the *Daily Racing Form*.

"I've got Mischief in the sixth race to win. Sure bet, right?" asked Russo's new best friend.

On cue, two men dressed in black suits took seats behind Russo. Two others emerged at the rail in front of him.

Russo had grown immune to paranoia and, for that matter, thinking about how his life might end abruptly. But these goons weren't goodfellas. If they were, he'd be dead already. They had to be cops.

The muscular FBI agent in full Tampa attire pulled his Glock from his pants and held it at C. J.'s head with both hands. Another agent yanked Russo up by his collar, patted him down, and handcuffed him. Then C. J. Russo heard the words that evaded him for decades:

"Charles John Russo, also known as Charles John Carabbia Jr., you are under arrest for the murders of Lou Epperson and Michael Panessa and for conspiring against the government of the United States. Anything you say may be used against you…"

Caught at last, C. J. Russo had only one thing to say. "What took you guys so long?"

* * *

Six hundred and sixty miles away across the northern shoreline of the Gulf of Mexico, the party in the Big Easy was just getting started.

After decades with Sykes Corp. that included an unpleasant stint in godforsaken Youngstown, Landon Daumbrelle managed to outlive the company's founders—the disreputable Sykes brothers—and his mentor/father-in-law, Jennings Landry. Daumbrelle's survival skills, including his exaggerated social standing, brought him to the moment he had long awaited.

Bad times had befallen the corrupt Sykes Corp. Stripped of government subsidies, Sykes sold what remained of its steel properties. Its troubled shipping line was sinking. To assert control over its more diversified business empire—malls, property, and agribusiness in Florida—the Sykes family announced it would move its headquarters from New Orleans to Tampa. Landon Daumbrelle was assigned to stay behind to memorialize the Sykes legacy. With nothing to do, he decided to throw a coming-out party for himself.

There was no more appropriate place to honor New Orleans's haughty kingfish than from his favorite pond, Commander's Palace, the iconic restaurant in the Garden District. Daumbrelle reserved the room overlooking the garden for his celebration. The problem was that no one in New Orleans business community, nor anyone in the city's cultivated social circles, wanted anything to do with the pompous buffoon left behind by a retreating company.

Landon opted for a public display of excess. He reserved the prized corner table in the Garden Room, the seen-and-be-seen alcove where the cultured and influential dined. There, he set a feast and waited for the city's other commanders to come by and pay homage at his table.

Collaborating with Ms. Ella, the matriarch of New Orleans's celebrated restaurant scene, Landon prepared for a long evening of tributes by ordering lavishly: four courses with multiple choices set in the middle of the always-elegant, always-booked Garden Room. Haute New Awlins and *trés coûteux*—very pricey:

There were the appetizers: Gulf jumbo shrimp with tasso ham, buttermilk-crusted chicken livers with cognac pâté, and oysters from Plaquemines Parish with choupique caviar.

There were two soup courses: turtle soup (the Commander's classic that takes three days to make) finished tableside with aged sherry and gumbo in a dark roux of the Cajun holy trinity and rum barrel hot sauce.

There were three entrees to impress: spiced peach and honey-glazed quail stuffed with Creole boudin and rum barrel kimchi, pecan-roasted Gulf redfish with jumbo lump crab, and Lake Pontchartrain soft-shell crab.

The dessert table overflowed with the city's signature sweets: bread pudding soufflé; a whiskey-soaked corn biscuit with Creole cream cheese known as Jamie cake; and bananas foster flambé, a sweet legacy of New Orleans's once-booming banana trade.

It was a menu to make the city's elite take notice. *I will impress them all,* Landon vowed. *I will win them over.*

Lauryn Coates was the first and only guest to make her way to Daumbrelle's corner table.

"I'm afraid I've crashed your party, Mr. Daumbrelle," she said apologetically, arriving at a table overstuffed with food and wine. "My name is Lauryn Coates."

"I don't think I've made your acquaintance, Ms. Coates," Daumbrelle said politely. "Nor do I detect a New Awlins accent. What brings you to my table?"

"I'm here to arrest you, sir."

"Arrest me? How charming. What exactly did I do to warrant such attention?"

"You killed a man, perpetrated a cover-up, and participated in a conspiracy against the United States government."

"Oh my, that sounds quite despicable," Daumbrelle replied. "Unfortunately, you are obviously confused about your whereabouts, Ms. Coates. Look about you. There are no murderers or conspirators in this elegant room. If there are, they will eat very well at my expense."

"We'll see that you get the bill," Coates said agreeably. "In the meantime, I'd advise you to come with me to avoid a scene."

"And why would I do that, dear girl?"

"Let's start again," Coates said, pulling out her shield. "My name is Lauryn Coates. I am a special agent for the Federal Bureau of Investigation. You are under arrest for the murder of Lou Epperson in Youngstown, Ohio, in 1977. Please come with me quietly, or I will have you removed in handcuffs."

"You remove me? I don't think so."

"Then I should introduce you to the rest of my dinner party," Coates explained. "The men and women sitting at the tables on either side of you are also FBI agents."

One by one, four agents displayed their FBI shields. A fifth waved a jumbo shrimp at Daumbrelle.

"You seem to have me at a disadvantage, Agent Coates," Daumbrelle admitted. Realizing that he was cornered, he suddenly panicked, bolting from his table to try to flee the room. He escaped only as far as the dessert table. There, four FBI agents pinned him facedown in New Orleans's best desserts. The fifth agent had already drawn his sidearm and pointed it at the self-anointed raconteur whose face was buried in the bread pudding.

Sticking her knee in Daumbrelle's back, Special Agent Lauryn Coates handcuffed him from behind and turned her head to the startled patrons in the Garden Room.

"Pardon us for disrupting your evening," she announced to the room, holding the host down on the dessert table. "The dinner is on Mr. Daumbrelle. Please continue dining, but one suggestion: I'd pass on the soufflé."

Then she lowered her head to the haughty host, his face covered in a goo of saturated bread, egg, molasses, and bourbon. The special agent brought her mouth to Daumbrelle's ear, licked a daub of the bread pudding from his lobe, and whispered the message she brought to New Orleans:

"Ms. LouAnn Epperson sends regrets that she's unable to attend your party."

Pulling her prisoner to his feet, Special Agent Lauryn Coates read the disgraced executive his rights. It was at that moment that Commander Landon Daumbrelle wet his seersucker suit for all the New Orleans luminaries in the palace to see.

PERSONAL TECHNOLOGY

A ping from the iPhone signaled the delivery of a text message. "Your ride is here," said the message from a source identified as the Timekeeper. Jordan Maier had learned to heed obscure signals across time. The reporter followed his nose to the faculty lot on the Youngstown State University campus. There he spotted an unmistakable vehicle: a gold 1976 Oldsmobile Cutlass coupe.

Lou Epperson's Cutlass from another time. Oh, why not.

Jordan climbed behind the wheel; the key was in the ignition. Another ping. This time the iPhone screen displayed a map and a route.

"Proceed to the route," a computer-generated voice instructed. Jordan didn't need directions; he recognized the destination immediately. Six minutes later by the time on his iPhone's GPS system, he pulled the vintage Cutlass to the gate of what was once the Brier Hill Works, now a desolate field of rubble surrounded by a rusting perimeter fence.

"We've been expecting you, Mr. Maier," the guard at the security shack said. "Just follow the road past the old shipping yard and park around back. You'll see the entrance at the loading docks."

Jordan knew the way. Only one structure remained from the demolition of the steel mills up and down the Mahoning. From the outside, the structure looked like a surviving outpost from the industrial apocalypse. The words *Youngstown Steel*, painted long ago on the side of the structure, disappeared into a mere suggestion. Only the letters spelling *Youngstow* could be discerned. The final n and the word *Steel* were gone.

Something about the structure didn't look quite right. Gutted from the inside, it should have been a shell, open at the ends from the removal of huge steelmaking equipment and the looting of the interior. The factory windows along the roofline should have been broken out. Instead, there were dark windows that blended with the smoke-stained roofline and walls.

As instructed, Jordan followed the gravel road to the back of the building. There he spotted the door on an elevated landing between two loading docks. Parking the Cutlass at the dock, he headed for the door. He stopped in his tracks when he spotted the words painted on weathered, corrugated steel: Half-Light Technologies.

This must be some kind of cruel joke. What? Who?

The answer arrived when LouAnn Epperson walked through the door.

LouAnn was a vision. Older, of course, but more striking and poised than Jordan remembered. She wore a perfectly tailored pant-suit. Her silk blouse was unbuttoned just enough to tease. Jordan recalled the moment when he put his mouth on that part of LouAnn's anatomy, recalling her words precisely.

"Perhaps you've set your sights a little too high."

"Don't say a word," LouAnn said, indulging the fantasy. "Just follow me."

Through the door, the lobby of Half-Light Technologies was spartan, dominated by a Formica counter that stretched across the back of the room. A security guard, disguised by the Dickies work clothes he wore, sat behind the counter operating what appeared to be a boxy outdated computer. A door into the factory was positioned on the unadorned wall behind the counter.

"I'll have your iPhone," the guard said.

Jordan balked.

"Don't worry. You'll get it back," LouAnn assured him.

Jordan gave it up. The lobby agent placed the iPhone in a dock that uploaded additional applications into the device, returning it to Jordan when the programming was quickly completed.

"Watch me." LouAnn held her iPhone to a pad that activated a screen positioned at eye level next to the door, staring into it as it scanned her face—facial recognition. "You're next." She smiled at Jordan as she walked into a chamber, the door closing behind her.

Jordan passed the face test, too, and entered the chamber where LouAnn was waiting for him. "I know you have questions, but wait, just wait," she implored. "There's something I must do first."

She kissed him passionately.

"In the half-light of morning," Jordan whispered in the embrace that followed.

"Something like that. It's our cover story…but not exactly our secret anymore," LouAnn said, holding Jordan tightly as she glanced into the camera mounted on the ceiling of the chamber.

Breaking away, LouAnn moved to the end of the chamber and inserted the badge hanging from her neck into a card reader mounted on the back wall. The back wall opened, revealing the hidden operations of so-called Half-Light Technologies.

The inside of the abandoned steel factory had been transformed into an elaborate technological city. A central corridor ran down the middle of the steel plant's vast interior, a path defined by a huge obsolete overhead crane painted bright yellow. The signature "Jonny Mann" was painted on it.

"Is it?"

"The same," LouAnn interrupted. "He died a few years ago."

"Steelworker's disease: pancreatic cancer," Jordan added. "I wrote his obit."

The concourse was flanked on both sides by sealed offices that looked as if they were transported from a space station. On one side of the corridor, the second level was open to the roof of the original steel mill. An industrial loft contained dozens of workstations and desks topped with computer screens, techies positioned behind all of them. The second level on the opposite side of the corridor was enclosed by glass—a command center with flat-paneled monitors visible behind the glass.

The corridor led to a circular amphitheater—the hub of the enclosed city. A large semi-circular projection screen wrapped around the back half of the amphitheater; steps formed the other half of the circle, cascading down to a platform—a town center. A few techies sat on cushions on the steps circling the screen. They linked their laptops and mobile devices to multiple sections of data and images that were displayed on the screen. Others worked on their laptops at tables in the adjoining café.

LouAnn stopped at a coffee bar, poured two cups, and set them on a café table at the edge of an atrium where a bamboo forest, a pond, and Japanese garden had been installed on the riverside of the old steel mill, separated from the Mahoning by a wall of one-way glass.

Sipping coffee and talking like ordinary people, LouAnn and Jordan could have been mistaken for a couple in a park. But unlike normal couples, they were destined to take comfort in brief tender mercies distributed across time and a painful past. As with all their moments, this one would be short and intense, leaving both of them vulnerable, fragile, and hurt.

Jordan was trying to understand. At the back end of the mill, he spotted a cluster of converted cargo containers, stacked one on top of the other—part avant-garde sculpture, part industrial-utopian apartment building.

"Sorry about the cliché, but I've a feeling we're not in Kansas anymore," he said, recalling the oft-cited line from *The Wizard of Oz*.

"Behold the Emerald City," LouAnn said proudly, describing the enclosed city-lab with shops, cafés, housing, and computer stations for sixty live-in inhabitants. "Actually, it's called the Cave—Community for Adaptive Vision Everywhere."

"How long have you been here, oh, Oz, the great and powerful," Jordan mocked.

"About a year."

"Excuse me. Did you say *about* a year?" the visitor asked.

"Yes, about a year," LouAnn answered.

"About a year," he repeated calmly, momentarily suppressing his incredulity. "You abandon me—that makes twice. Then you hide for a year in your secret fortress of solitude just a few miles away? *A year? A fucking year?*"

LouAnn didn't appreciate the tone from a so-called observant reporter who somehow failed to notice that a secret city was built right under his nose.

"Yes, about a year," she said unapologetically. "Now, stop playing the victim and listen.

"I know I'm not the wizard you expected, but I might be the wizard that you need. Isn't that from the movie too? This is not a movie set, Jordan. Let's start with that."

"This ought to be good," came the insincere reply.

Starting with Caltech and the government-sponsored infotech lab, LouAnn described a journey that included secret projects with her SMUG colleagues at the Jet Propulsion Lab, Sun Microsystems, Oracle, Google, Qualcomm, Apple, and Northrop Grumman—all under the auspices of DARPA.

"Terrorism changed the game," she explained. "After 9/11, we began to develop the new weapons and information systems. Make no mistake: the nation's defense is fortified by information. I can't say more, Jordan, but you have to understand. I wanted to see you, but I couldn't. It would have put both of us at risk."

The explanation worked. Jordan felt suddenly foolish. "And this place?"

"A secure bunker for intelligence and the development of advanced intelligence systems. We apply emerging waves of technology—capabilities that seem unimaginable—to our nation's defense systems."

Technology was to the twenty-first century what fossil fuels and manufactured metals were to the Industrial Age. Constantly measured and priced, emerging technologies spurred the growth of economies built on a foundation of terabytes and gigabits per second. What better place than a converted steel mill in Youngstown for the

Timekeeper's daughter to reconcile the ironies of time? Youngstown had become invisible in the current epoch—the perfect cover for an advanced intelligence operation.

"There's no place like home," LouAnn quipped. "We're not far from Washington yet remote in our location and context. No one pays attention to the rubble in this part of town anymore. You're seeing what we've been able to accomplish here without attracting attention."

"So this is your idea?" he asked.

"My idea. My project."

"Then I have another question: What am I doing here?"

"You're here to tell our story."

"Oh, good, manipulation," Jordan said, cynicism returning.

"You'll be interested in what I have to show you. You can decide what to do with it. But first, I want to hear about you."

The skeptical reporter wasn't about to be patronized by the tech goddess. "No you don't. You want something from me again," he said. "But hey, I'll play along since you've gone to so much trouble."

Pausing, Jordan considered his mediocre career, comparing it to the one of the universally significant LouAnn Epperson.

"Okay, LouAnn, here's my LinkedIn version," he allowed. "You left. I stayed. I became disillusioned with *The Examiner*, and *The Examiner* had had enough of me. So I launched a blog, appropriately called it *The Ex*, and with predictable cynicism, agreed to teach digital journalism at YSU. Now I spend my time trying to teach word-impaired teenagers how to write a serviceable sentence about the real world while they play World of Warcraft on their mobile devices. Not exactly the stuff of making the world safe from terrorism, is it?"

LouAnn was enamored by the circle of circumstance that brought Jordan back to their college days.

"I love that you're back at the place where we started, Billy Pilgrim," she said. "I love that you're teaching. And I love that you're a better journalist than you've ever been."

"Why I am not surprised that you know all this? And how did you find me on campus?"

"I've followed you," LouAnn admitted. "And now I'm about to show you something that will make World of Warcraft seem like Pong."

Jordan tried to process it all. "Why am I here, LouAnn? I have a feeling that it doesn't have to do with college days or our screwed-up relationship. That kiss in the security room…you know it could be considered sexual harassment."

"Not unless my sexual advances were unwanted," LouAnn teased. "Were they?"

For all the incredible things he had seen in the past thirty minutes and for all the remarkable stories he had heard, Jordan couldn't help but fixate on LouAnn's question. The sexual tension between them spanned time and place. Out of nowhere, the Timekeeper's daughter materializes in a secret operation of global importance in a converted steel mill in Youngstown. And all Jordan could think about was the reunion they planned later at the cottage.

LINGUA FRANCA

At a top secret demonstration in 1969, technologists at the US Defense Department's lavishly funded research arm set the Information Revolution in motion. It was ten years after one of the most dramatic moments in the cold war. With technology accelerating rapidly, the Soviet Union launched an intercontinental ballistic missile (ICBM); the world's first satellite, Sputnik 1; and the world's second satellite, Sputnik 2. The Advanced Research Projects Agency (ARPA) was formed with urgency. By 1969, a computer network called Arpanet linked mainframes at universities, government agencies, and defense contractors around the country. Arpanet was the beginning of a global system of interconnected computer networks—a network of networks—known as the Internet.

Internetworking was the problem that a young computer scientist at Caltech was recruited to unravel. It presented enormous challenges. Getting computers to talk to one another—networking—had been hard enough. But getting networks to talk to one another—internetworking—posed a whole new set of difficulties because the networks spoke alien and incompatible languages. Trying to move data from one to another was like writing a letter in Mandarin to someone who only knows Farsi and hoping to be understood.

By the time LouAnn Epperson's preliminary research in applied computer linguistics had begun, ARPA had added a D to its name, but the complexity of interworking had grown exponentially. New formats were added to the vocabulary of the Internet, not just the ones and zeros of data but also the pixels of images and the lines of appearing and disappearing pixels in moving visual media—data only seen in glimpses. Additionally, there was the data that was unseen, the essence of cyberspace that, like faith, exists without tangible form on the computer screen.

LouAnn's talent, her undeniable brilliance, was to develop a kind of digital Esperanto: a common language that enabled data to be understood in any format, a universal set of rules to understand what computers were telling us.

LouAnn future-proofed a language that grew infinitely with each node on the Internet, each new technology leapfrogging the previous. The enemy changed, too, as did the geography. After 9/11, DARPA turned to her to decode terrorism, a threat to Western civilization greater than the Soviet missiles and satellites of the cold war era.

LouAnn Epperson would develop the lingua franca of the dark web for DARPA. The software she developed became the tool to decipher what was said and seen everywhere. She called the software the Language Optimization Utility—LOU.|

* * *

"If a picture is worth a thousand words, then a video is worth a thousand pictures."

LouAnn went straight to the point in a demonstration that, not unlike the Arpanet demonstration in 1969, would push the Information Revolution forward with an interpretive lens on the static and dynamic images on the Internet.

She proceeded without introducing the four people who were brought to a high-tech briefing room in a converted steel plant in Youngstown, Ohio. The circumstances were just too bizarre to explain.

Three people linked in on a secure satellite transmission channel: Special Agent Lauryn Coates, head of the FBI's Criminal, Cyber, Response, and Services Branch; Lionel Koda, Deputy Assistant

Attorney General for the Justice Department's Antitrust Division; and Christina Duncan, the director of DARPA.

Coates was linked to the briefing from an FBI field office in New Orleans, Koda from Justice Department offices on Pennsylvania Avenue on the National Mall, and Duncan from DARPA's headquarters across the Potomac in Arlington near the Pentagon. Their faces appeared on a single video screen, names and locations appearing under a caption on the screen that said, "Secure Video Transmission, Level 2, NROL-27 (SDS-3), designating the level of security for the transmission and the government satellite that enabled it.

The fourth guest in the room was Jordan Maier, a local blogger and part-time college teacher, the only person besides LouAnn who was physically present. He had no idea why he was there, only that he was in way over his head.

LouAnn looked through Jordan, making him feel all the more insignificant. Holding a video cassette liberated from a steel plant, this place, in 1979, she refreshed his memory of an escapade that almost cost him his job. "As you'll recall, Mr. Maier, this cassette was sent to Caltech. You're probably interested in what it shows."

Mr. Maier? I must have really pissed off LouAnn. Now the feds are going to bust me for aiding and abetting the removal of stolen property from a long-abandoned steel plant years ago.

Fortunately, LouAnn—herself an accomplice—skipped the details of acquiring the cassette and moved straight to the point: "Our initial problem was that the eyewitness to the incident in the Brier Hill Works—this video—wasn't speaking a language we could understand."

"On screen," she ordered. Responding to her voice command, one frame of the video was projected across an entire glass wall in the briefing room known as the Holodeck. An image of the interior shipping yard at the old Brier Hill Works was displayed across one wall.

"As you can see, the resolution is quite poor because we were dealing with nascent technology from a Japanese manufacturer. It's as if we've just discovered the Dead Sea scrolls in a cave. How does one extract relevant meaning from manuscripts written in Hebrew,

Aramaic, and Greek dating to 400 BCE? The Brier Hill video presents a similar problem. Let's try to interpret it."

"The video camera was mounted about right here," LouAnn continued, pointing to a barely discernible black box mounted on the dark underside of an overhead crane. "Let me orient you: that spot in the shipping mill is almost right above me."

"Lou Epperson's office is over here, just past the stacks of steel plates," she continued, gesturing to the small office on the upper corner of the screen. "That would be down the corridor from where I'm standing now, in the back corner of the plate yard, next to a corridor leading to what was then the blooming mill."

The earliest portable video cameras had to be connected to a tape machine in order to work. LouAnn explained that the cassette was first shown on a television screen connected to a video player. Since then, the video had since been digitized so its content could be displayed and analyzed by computer software. "Run the video," came her next voice command.

The video opened with a fuzzy, distant shot of Lou Epperson seated in an office where the front and side walls were glass from the middle up. Columns of steel plates, stacked high on palettes, obscured most of the frame. Two men emerged from the stacks, one wearing a gray suit with a red pocket scarf, the other dressed all in black. Each of the men wore hard hats. The two men appeared to confront Lou Epperson, who rose and pointed to the door. Visibly, the video appeared to suggest that words were exchanged, but they could not be heard due to the distance of the camera and the din of operations in the steel mill. The two men didn't move until Epperson pushed past. They followed him out of the office and disappeared behind the stacks of steel plates.

Several seconds passed without discernible activity on the tape. Then a hard hat, separated from the head that had occupied it, could be seen rolling on the floor between two stacks of steel.

The man dressed in black was then seen emerging from the stacks, moving toward the office. He dragged a body by the feet. He was followed by the man in the gray suit, who was no longer wearing a hard hat but carried one as he followed the man in the black suit. All three disappeared into a dark corridor outside the office.

"The video was turned over to the FBI," LouAnn explained. "I'll let Special Agent Coates take it from there."

On her video link, Coates picked up the cue. "Using the technology that was available at the time, the FBI's Criminal, Cyber, Response, and Services Branch determined there was a scuffle, but it was obscured by the stacks of steel plates. The identities of the man in all black and the one in the gray suit could not be determined due to the poor quality of the video and the distance from which the incident was recorded. Moreover, there was no physical evidence to suggest that a crime had taken place."

"You mean other than the body in the steel mill?" Jordan challenged, no longer intimidated by the powers in the briefing.

"The video was deemed inclusive by the FBI," Coates said calmly. "There was no evidence of a crime. No case. The company ruled that their employee was killed in an industrial accident."

"An industrial accident the FBI didn't even bother to check it out," Jordan railed. "You guys couldn't hit water if you fell out of a boat."

Coates was offended now. "Be careful, Mr. Maier," she said. "Let me remind you of three facts: The first is that I've agreed to be here in order to help you. The second is that the video was stolen property. The third is that you have not heard the complete story."

Jordan should have kept his mouth shut, but decades-long frustration made him stupid. "What are going to do? Arrest me for improper video sharing?"

The FBI agent couldn't resist. "Well, actually, we considered taking you on a Youngstown joyride and beating the crap out of you. Fortunately for you, our interrogation methods have become more scientific."

Reliant on the FBI's cooperation, LouAnn thought it was a good time to diplomatically intervene. "Actually, Jordan, we're here because of you," she said. "We're getting off point. Deputy Assistant Attorney General Koda can take it from here. Mr. Koda, I believe you are acquainted with Mr. Maier."

Lionel Koda certainly was.

KODA

It was Lionel Koda's role to bring sense to the intertwined abstractions that led to the murder of a whistleblower, a government conspiracy that hastened the demise of industrial America, and the series of unforeseen events in Youngstown that altered the lives of a reporter, a computer scientist, tens of thousands of steelworkers, and the 150,000 residents of a steel town.

Koda was a career bureaucrat, a dogged investigator promoted up the ranks of the Justice Department's most boring, do-nothing, career-busting division—Antitrust. But for the *k* instead of the *c* beginning his last name, he was perfectly identified. It was his nature to round out, conclude, and summarize complex interactions that led to foregone conclusions, mostly those that served the interests of the current administration. In the language of his tribe, the Dakota of the northern Mississippi Valley, *koda* translated as "the ally." From a communications link that spanned eras, the Ally sought to provide context to a twisted tale.

"We meet again, Mr. Maier," Koda said on the video transmission. "If I recall correctly, we talked in 1978 about the process for filing a Freedom of Information Act request for the release of government documents pertaining to the Youngstown Steel mergers. Time has passed."

As a young antitrust lawyer, Koda headed the staff investigation into Sykes Corp.'s acquisition of Youngstown Steel, as well as the subsequent merger proposed between Youngstown Steel and Jones

& Laughlin Steel. He was present when Youngstown Steel president Jennings Lambert made his case to Attorney General Winston Dell.

"It was shortly thereafter that I became acquainted with your reporting, Mr. Maier," Koda explained. "Our staff investigation determined that Youngstown Steel was not a failing company and, thus, did not meet the failing company exception that would justify a merger. The attorney general thought otherwise. But you know that. What you don't know is that I read your story in *The Youngstown Examiner* three days later, the story that ran under the headline 'Death of the Timekeeper.' Perhaps you remember?"

Like it was yesterday.

Koda didn't wait for Jordan to articulate his thought: "Your story was affirming, enlightening, and—I'm sorry to say—tragic. It revealed that Lou Epperson—whom you call 'the Timekeeper'—was the whistleblower who was supplying the Antitrust Division's investigative staff with inventory records that showed that Youngstown Steel's business was healthy. Three days after the meeting between Youngstown Steel execs and the attorney general, Mr. Epperson was dead."

"And that didn't set off alarms?" Jordan asked the image on the screen.

"Actually, it did, Mr. Maier," Koda acknowledged. "In situations such as this, Justice goes into stealth mode. We are advised not to draw conclusions, not to issue statements, to keep our heads down. It is an institutional condition known as plausible deniability."

"The decision about the merger was a foregone conclusion," Koda elaborated. "The next move was to distance the administration from events. In the scheme of public policy, Youngstown had become a mosquito. I can recall Attorney General Dell's exact words: 'Mosquitoes bite you as if they are in some kind of love with you.' I repeat that colorful characterization with impunity, of course."

Jordan gave voice to his next thoughts. "So the thinking at the top levels of government was that since Youngstown was insignificant and that no one outside Youngstown gave a damn, a homicide and the demise of a city would simply go away with time."

"That's about right," Koda said. "But there was only one problem."

"What's that?" Jordan asked.

"You," Koda revealed.

"You mean a clueless cub reporter from an insignificant, second-rate newspaper in Smoke Stack, USA," Jordan clarified.

"We didn't see you coming," Koda admitted. "We underestimated you."

"Now you're lying, Mr. Koda," Jordan challenged. "You didn't underestimate me. You played me perfectly. Your miscalculation was underestimating the daughter of a murder victim who just happens to be smarter than everyone in this room."

"Fortunately, that is the case," Koda said.

Jordan tried to process Koda's surprising admission. How did this web of deceit lead to a mock hearing in a secret bunker for military intelligence? "I still don't get it," Jordan said. "So let me ask this again: What am I doing here? Why now?"

Then came the voice from the only other person who was physically in the room.

"I'll take it from here," LouAnn Epperson said.

OBJECTIVE REALITY

In 1982, a small group of scientists gathered at the University of Paris for one of the most important experiments of the twentieth century. A research team led by physicist Alain Aspect discovered that under certain circumstances, subatomic particles such as electrons are able to instantaneously communicate with each other regardless of the distance separating them. It doesn't matter whether they are ten feet or ten billion miles apart. Somehow, each particle seems to know what the other is doing.

The experiment did not make the evening news. But for a few scientific journals, it was barely reported at all. Few in the small club of physicists had even heard of Alain Aspect. And they had a problem: his experiment contradicted Einstein's long-held tenet that no communication can travel faster than the speed of light.

Since traveling faster than the speed of light is tantamount to breaking the time barrier, this daunting prospect caused some scientists to try to come up with elaborate ways to explain away Aspect's findings. It inspired others to offer even more radical explanations. LouAnn Epperson was one of them. She reasoned that objective reality may not exist. Despite its apparent solidity, the universe is a phantasm, a gigantic and splendidly detailed hologram.

LouAnn's ambition was not to change the face of science but rather to use science to better understand reality. Aspect's discovery of the apparent faster-than-light connection between subatomic particles told her that there is a deeper level of reality that we are not

184

privy to. She embarked on a scientific quest to explain reality with holograms.

Large-scale holograms, illuminated with lasers or displayed in a darkened room with a carefully directed beam of light, are two-dimensional surfaces that show precise three-dimensional images of real objects. If you look at these holograms from different angles, you see objects from different perspectives, just like you would if you were looking at a real object. Some holograms even appear to move as you walk past them and look at them from different angles.

LouAnn's ability to see and foster connections between seemingly disparate fields of science brought her to the secret DARPA facility in Youngstown at this moment in time. That and the unresolved matter with her father, the Timekeeper. As a child, her father taught her to see by observing the visual world with its countless objects and scenes. As a computer scientist, she reasoned that computers could learn in similar ways by analyzing a wide variety of images and the relationships between them.

This was the thinking that caused LouAnn to convert a first-generation video of an obscured decades-old incident in a steel plant into a hologram that revealed objective reality: indisputable evidence of an old crime.

* * *

"Let's have another look at that video," she suggested in the empty room known as the Holodeck.

She clicked the mobile device she held in one hand, and a still image of the original video reappeared on one wall. "Run it again," she commanded by voice. Replayed, the video showed the same vague sequence of events with men in hard hats moving behind stacks of steel plates, apparently—but not definitively—to settle a dispute. Seconds passed, and once more, a hard hat could be seen rolling in the space between the stacks.

"What did we just see?" LouAnn asked. "Not much. We were looking for a story that unfolded behind tons of steel. We should have been looking at a window into the real story. Here."

LouAnn pointed to a smudge on the window in the corner office. "A dirty window in a grimy mill? Not unexpected. Look closer. It appears to be a faint reflection or, more precisely, what scientists call a refraction: the change of direction that light undergoes when it enters a medium with a different density from the one through which it has been traveling. What that means is that there's a story in the window that we can decipher."

The hidden story was about to unfold in a three-dimensional video made by bending subatomic particles of light.

"The story in the smudge begins when Lou Epperson activates a video camera he installed under the carriage of overhead crane that is located about one hundred feet away," LouAnn explained. "It is at that moment that the camera begins to capture a crime that is refracted on the office window."

LouAnn then gave a voice command that transformed the room: "Start projection."

It was if a room-sized curtain had been raised revealing a three-dimensional stage that wrapped around the walls, ceiling, and floor of the Holodeck. Lou Epperson's office and the back corridor of the plate mill were projected, larger than life, in the center of the hologram that filled the room. Three-dimensional images of Lou Epperson, Landon Daumbrelle, and C. J. Russo were projected in positions that corresponded to their places in the original two-dimensional video. The stage unfolded around LouAnn and Jordan, the only two physical forms in the room, who were seated on stools close enough to touch the objects and players in the projection.

The scene from the smudge provided a perfect angle to witness events that had eluded explanation for decades:

Attempting to leave his office, Lou Epperson was confronted by Russo and Daumbrelle. Words were exchanged, although sound was not captured in the original video. Daumbrelle became agitated and then threatening, grabbing Epperson by his collar. As they scuffed,

Daumbrelle shoved the plant superintendent. Epperson grabbed Daumbrelle's red pocket scarf as he fell backward into the corner of steel plates. His hard hat flew off as he struck his head on the corner of the plate stack, causing Epperson to fall to the ground unconscious, still holding the red pocket scarf. Russo became enraged, shouting at Daumbrelle. Russo dropped to his knees, put his ear to Epperson's heart, and then turned to say something to Daumbrelle. Then the two of them picked up Lou Epperson's body and dragged it into the darkness of a corridor that lead to the soaking pits. The fall didn't kill Lou Epperson. He died, unconscious, in the bottom of a pit, breathing fumes from the acids and chemicals that saturated the tomb.

Russo returned a few moments later to wipe up a small amount of blood on the floor. He used the red pocket scarf, which he stuffed into his pants pocket.

"End projection."

LouAnn had seen the Holodeck projection numerous times in recent days and many times more in countless versions displayed in lesser technologies over the years. Her long experiment in scientific forensics complete, she brought her hands together in a prayerlike gesture, brought them to her mouth, and bowed her head.

"Perhaps I should speak now," came the voice from a video monitor.

"First, I should put a piece of evidence into perspective," said Special Agent Coates. "Over the years, Mr. Russo kept the red pocket scarf in his possession to link Mr. Daumbrelle to Lou Epperson's murder. Upon his arrest, the scarf was turned over to the FBI. DNA testing confirmed that it belonged to Mr. Daumbrelle and that is was saturated with Lou Epperson's blood."

Next, Coates moved to the arrests. "Landon Daumbrelle and C. J. Russo were arrested yesterday in New Orleans and Tampa, respectively, for the murder of Lou Epperson in 1977," she announced. "The circumstances revealed in the hologram projection that we just saw provided conclusive evidence that had eluded the FBI for decades. Additionally, a conspiracy involving the nation's steel industry and the Antitrust Division of the US Justice Department was exposed as part of our investigation.

"These arrests end a disturbing chapter in our nation's progress. They could not have been achieved without LouAnn Epperson, who worked tirelessly and, I should say, brilliantly across time and technologies to achieve justice, not just for those responsible her father's death but for the defense and security of our nation.

"We recognize, too, Mr. Maier, that you played a determining role in exposing crime and corruption at the highest levels of industry and government. For that, you, too, deserve our appreciation. We express that today by providing you with this exclusive briefing on the arrests and the investigation. Do you have any questions?"

Only one occurred to Jordan: "What took so long?"

Lauryn Coates just shook her head and signed off.

* * *

Left alone in the surreal world of an abandoned steel plant that was converted into a DARPA technology installation, LouAnn and Jordan confronted the confusing irony of their past and present. They reflected until LouAnn broke the silence.

"If you're going to ask me how I feel, I'm going to call security and have you tortured."

"You have that kind of power?" Jordan asked.

"You have no idea," LouAnn replied, still contemplative. "I failed, Jordan."

"You failed?" Jordan asked incredulously. "I know you're prone to exceeding expectations and overcoming discrimination by all manners of assholes, but you just solved a decades-old murder, uncovered a government conspiracy, validated your father's abiding faith in you, and—oh, by the way—invented technology that changes the way society can see and interpret details and motives from any place in this world. You're probably going to win the Nobel Prize for something, LouAnn. And the prize won't come close to recognizing the full extent of your achievement. Look around you."

"Lights and shadows, subatomic particles arranged to create someone's version of objective reality. That's all. The truth is that I don't believe in objective reality," LouAnn admitted.

"What exactly *do* you believe in?" Jordan asked.

"Faces and voices," LouAnn replied. "Forty thousand steelworkers were displaced here. My father was murdered here. An era ended here. I have committed all the faces and voices to a tomb."

"What about your voice? What does it tell you?"

LouAnn considered the questions and recalled her return to Youngstown in 1977.

"There's one more video that I must play for you, Billy Pilgrim," she said. "I've had it since that day when I called you from the cottage. My father left it for me in our secret hiding place, a compartment in a child's dollhouse that could only be opened by the wooden crosses that my father and I wore around our necks. He would leave prizes in the compartment—books, handwritten haiku, trinkets, or the precious little charms treasured by little girls. I only had to unlock the hidden compartment by twisting my cross into a key that solved the puzzle of the lock. On that terrible day, I unlocked our secret compartment to discover the videotape that the Youngstown Steel goons were so desperate to discover."

"Play the Timekeeper tape," she instructed the voice-enabled computer.

The projection of the steel mill corridor that filled the Holodeck disappeared, leaving the room empty and dark. A flickering white frame appeared on the back wall. Then came a close-up shot—a crude, amateur, predigital selfie from Lou Epperson that struck Jordan as eerie. The Timekeeper spoke directly to his daughter from the prototype video equipment he brought home from Japan:

"My brilliant LouAnn, let's get the abstractions out of the way first. The fact that you are watching this video means that certain unpleasant events have transpired.

"I have set these events in motion by attempting to prevent an offense against humanity. I have not succeeded. The circumstances of my failure are now becoming abundantly clear to you.

"The resolution of these events now falls on you. It will take time, a long time, to reconcile them. I know the task is unfair. Be as patient as you are brilliant. This is what you must understand: Just as technology makes things easier, it has the potential to handicap our connection with the world around us.

"Your mother, a teacher, understood this. You carry her spirit and her name as well as mine. You will hold yourself responsible for events that you cannot change. That only proves you are human. Follow your humanity. It is time for me to go. Goodbye for now."

The flickering image of the Timekeeper faded to white. Tears welled in LouAnn's eyes. "You see, Billy Pilgrim, I've failed," she said.

"I don't see how," Jordan said, attempting to console her.

"I create spyware for the Defense Department. I'm responsible for weaponizing technology," LouAnn despaired. "It's not as if I'm advancing humanity."

"Maybe you're not done yet," Jordan offered.

The idea caught LouAnn off guard, causing her to sort out conflicts swirling in her analytical mind. Jordan watched her methodically calculate a new scientific equation: whether technology would benefit or harm humanity.

"Many children, young adults, and even adults are having fewer and fewer human interactions, while their human-technology interactions are increasing," she explained, "Now we're developing artificial intelligence that will affect the way people work and live. It's bound to alter the human experience—and not necessarily for the better. We have time, but we have to act now. If we make fundamental changes to how AI is engineered—and who engineers it—the technology will be a transformative force for good. If not, we are leaving a lot of humanity out of the equation. So far, we have been unable to resolve the conflict between science and humanity. I think I understand why."

"Why?" Jordan asked.

"It takes a woman," the Timekeeper's daughter said.

RETURN TO CONTINUUM

Everything passes, but nothing entirely goes away. Jordan Maier returned to Continuum. He parked Lou Epperson's vintage Cutlass and sought refuge inside the cottage before the shadows swallowed it in darkness.

Something was different at the entry door. Jordan recalled the confrontation there between devils and gods. The rickety screen door that separated LouAnn from Youngstown Steel's goon squad so long ago had been replaced. So had the aged wooden door behind the screen. A new door made of steel provided security. Spotting the keypad that was affixed to the wall next to the door, Jordan knew what to do.

Recalling the access protocol he encountered earlier in the day, he pulled from his pocket the uber-programmed iPhone he was given. Holding the screen to the keypad, the door popped open.

Jordan's time-traveling moment was about to get stranger. Time bent forward inside the cottage. It was in shambles the first time he was inside, turned upside down by corporate thugs looking for incriminating evidence. LouAnn left it in disarray when she fled back to Pasadena. Years later, the interior had been modernized, the doors and windows upgraded and secured, and the hopelessly styleless 1970s period furnishings replaced with Crate & Barrel. An Apple PowerBook was placed on the dining room table, and security cameras were installed in the corners of room.

A motion sensor switched on the PowerBook as Jordan entered the dining room. He was greeted with the soothing computer-generated voice of Siri.

"It's good to have you back at Continuum, Jordan," Siri said. "I've opened a word-processing document for your story. May I help you with the lede?"

"I think I've got it covered. Thank you," Jordan replied.

"You are welcome," Siri continued. "Files from today's briefing have been loaded on your desktop. You may download them as needed."

Wasting no time, Jordan began to write. The keyboard could barely keep up with his fingers.

By Jordan Maier
jmaier@TheEx.com

YOUNGSTOWN, O.—A brilliant technologist, the daughter of a steel mill engineer, chased justice over time to solve a decades-long mystery that took the life of her beloved father, the whistleblower to a conspiracy. In doing so, the enigmatic computer scientist uncovered duplicitous dealings between high-ranking officials of the US government and executives from now-defunct Youngstown Steel to steer global markets for steel, shipping, and trade.

The disclosures came yesterday in Youngstown, a city devastated by the closing of its steel mills and the continuing decline of industrial America.

In New Orleans, federal agents arrested Landon Daumbrelle, the chief marketing officer of Sykes Corp. and a vice president of its former steel subsidiary, Youngstown Steel, for the 1977 murder of steelmaster Lou Epperson and the subsequent cover-up of the crime.

In Tampa, former Youngstown Steel security chief C. J. Russo was also arrested for the Epperson murder. Additionally, Russo was charged with the murder of shopping mall baron Michael Panessa, who was killed in 1979 when his private plane crashed following takeoff from his Boardman airstrip. Russo confessed to helping Daumbrelle cover up Lou Epperson's murder in Youngstown Steel's Brier Hill Works and to sabotaging Panessa's plane, according to the FBI.

Russo has been linked to organized crime families in Youngstown, New Orleans, and Tampa. He was arrested at Sunshine Downs in Tampa, a thoroughbred horse racing track where he currently serves as chief of security. "What took you so long?" he asked the FBI agents who arrested him.

Daumbrelle, a member of Sykes Corp.'s founding family, served as vice president of Youngstown Steel and Sykes Corp. during the mergers that consolidated the nation's steel industry. He is accused of killing Lou Epperson to prevent disclosure of evidence contradicting the "failing company" scenario on which the Youngstown Steel merger was based. He was arrested at a banquet he threw in his own behalf at Commander's Palace restaurant in New Orleans, a popular meeting spot in the Garden District for tourists, politicians, and local luminaries.

A former Youngstown Steel president, the late Jennings Landry, was also identified as a principal in the conspiracy and murder cases. Landry ran for congress in Louisiana in 1990 but was defeated following government disclosures that he was involved in the corporate scandals at Youngstown Steel and Sykes Corp. that rocked the nation's steel and shipping industries. He was reassigned to manage steel operations in Pittsburgh, where he lived in ignamy until his death in 2008.

Lou Epperson, also known as the Timekeeper, was murdered inside the Brier Hill Works on September 16, 1977, three days before Black Monday, the darkest day in Youngstown's history. Epperson, who supervised the Brier Hill Works, leaked damaging information to the government about Youngstown Steel's pending merger with Jones & Laughlin Steel. The details of the murder—ruled an industrial accident by Youngstown Steel at the time—remained a secret until yesterday, when advanced technology provided forensic evidence of the crime.

LouAnn Epperson, a researcher who heads an information technology lab at the California Institute of Technology, solved the mystery of her father's murder and its connection to the previously unknown scandal involving high-ranking officials of the Carter administration and top executives from the nation's steel and shipping companies.

The cases unfolded over years as scientific investigators applied generations of emerging technology to past evidence. The broad strokes of the investigations were revealed exclusively to *The Ex* yesterday at a secret facility for advanced research.

Daumbrelle and Landry, executives from the Youngstown Steel days, were implicated in the conspiracy to close the mills in the Steel Valley, a stunning act that ultimately cost 40,000 steel-workers their livelihoods and forever changed Youngstown's fortunes.

LouAnn Epperson's investigation, which began in 1979, was supported by a coalition of federal authorities and some of the world's most advanced technology companies. It found that top members of the Carter administration, including the late Attorney General Winston Dell and John Steverson, the chief of the Justice Department's Antitrust Division, were complicit in antitrust decisions involving mergers by Youngstown Steel; its parent company, the Sykes Corp.; and other major steel companies.

Waves of technological advance provided demonstrable evidence that cracked the cold case. Video taken at the time, advanced by information-age advances, took investigators back to the scene of Lou Epperson's murder. Nascent video taken in the Brier Hill Works in 1977 was analyzed by software and intelligence systems that showed Daumbrelle striking Epperson and Russo dragging his body away.

Daumbrelle, who is the son-in-law of the late Youngstown Steel president, and Russo stand accused of murdering Lou Epperson to silence him. At the time, Lou Epperson was believed to be a whistleblower who supplied the Justice Department's Antitrust Division with evidence that Youngstown Steel was not failing and thus did not meet conditions for its merger with Pittsburgh-based Jones & Laughlin Steel.

A champion of steelworkers in Youngstown, Lou Epperson's body was found in the bottom of an empty pit where steel products are tempered in an acid bath to remove impurities. His death was ruled accidental by Youngstown Steel at the time.

Three days later, Youngstown's aging steel mills were closed by Youngstown Steel to validate its "failing company" argument.

Youngstown was later regarded as a casualty of the nation's "steel wars" with Japan. US steel products and automobiles were placed in a competitive disadvantage with Japan, whose government subsidized its steel and auto industries.

Former Atty. Gen. Dell and Steverson, the Antitrust Division's chief attorney, were responsible for rulings on antitrust issues impacting national trade policy. In the 1970s, the federal government approved a series of corporate mergers that effectively doomed the nation's industrial legacy. In 1979, the Carter administration refused to fund the reopening of Youngstown's steel mills under community-worker ownership.

Winston Dell, who was the attorney general during most of the presidency of his friend Jimmy Carter, died in 2009 at the age of 90. John Steverson, 75, left the Justice Department following the Antitrust Division's approval of the Youngstown Steel merger. Steverson cooperated with federal investigators in return for immunity from prosecution, FBI investigators confirmed. He continues to advise corporations on antitrust matters from his prestigious law practice in Washington.

Meantime, LouAnn Epperson worked over four decades to solve her father's murder and unravel dealings between the federal government and US corporations that profited from policy decisions impacting the steel, shipping, and defense sectors. An information technologist relatively unknown outside of scientific circles, she used successive waves of advanced technology to uncover, analyze, and reinterpret original evidence.

LouAnn Epperson's technological brilliance and her scientific persistence led to yesterday's stunning disclosures. A graduate of Youngstown State University, she was the first woman to receive two doctorates, one in computer sciences, the other in information technologies, at the Massachusetts Institute of Technology in Cambridge, MA. She later founded the NexUs and Interdisciplinary Laboratory for Information Futures and Endeavors (iLIFE) at the California Institute of Technology in Pasadena, CA.

Little is known about LouAnn Epperson's work since then. Even those who know her regard her as an enigma.

There is a mix of emotions that reporters experience following the completion of a story long in the works—a curious blend of ego, pride, satisfaction tempered by self-doubt about the finality of publication, and fears about consequences. Depression frequently follows, haunting them.

Jordan had just written another obituary. Isolated in a secluded cottage located between then and now, he confronted uncertainty. He waited for LouAnn to arrive to make everything feel right again.

THE HALF-LIGHT OF MORNING

The only passenger on a private jet, LouAnn was fleeing again. She peered out the window, setting her sights on the horizon, searching for words, looking for meaning. The view returned darkness. She tried to conjure up the Timekeeper, but her memory brought only the haiku by Lauren Beukes in *The Shining Girls* that her father had long ago left for her in her dollhouse.

> She would disappear
> folded like origami
> into her own dreams

LouAnn clicked on her computer to atone for disappearing.

Jordan Maier's laptop clicked on simultaneously. The screen displayed the message "Secure Video Stream from LouAnn Epperson." An image of LouAnn appeared as Jordan peered into the small camera embedded in the computer above the screen.

"Looks like you figured out the gadgets," LouAnn said from the video window on her computer screen.

"You made it easy," came the reply from the other video window.

"Actually, the technology took decades to develop."

"We mortals can only imagine."

"Don't do that. I read your story. You're the only one who could have written that."

"And you look as if you're in an airplane. So where are you?"

"I really can't say."

"You mean you really *won't* say."

"I suppose that's right. Better if I'm not around when the story breaks. Besides, I have unfinished business."

"Of course…The brilliant scientist who pulls the levers at DARPA. The enigma. Must be complicated for you."

"Actually, it's better for you if I'm not there."

"Please explain that to me, LouAnn. What's your plan? To disappear only to conveniently drop in from time to time?"

"How can I explain? I've only loved three people: my father, my mother, and you. All of you are with me. You're all I've got."

"The sad part of that, LouAnn, is I'm the only one that's real in this existence, and I will end up loving you without you for much longer than I loved you when I knew you. Most people would find that strange."

"We're not like most people."

"So what then? I've always believed in the future, but not so much now. Now the past ceases to exist. For us, the past is everything."

"My love for you is not relative to the time I spend with you."

"That sounds like some ridiculous physics theory."

"LouAnn's theory of survival."

"Well, it's a black hole."

"I know, but it keeps me going…I have a proposition for you."

"Does it begin with the question 'Where are you Billy Pilgrim?'"

"Actually, yes. I want you to have the car and the cottage."

"I don't think I can unlock the security system at the front door again."

"No worries. I'll have the high-tech security locks removed. Who knows when I'll drop in?"

"You won't need your technologies to find me."

"I need you more than you know, Billy Pilgrim."

And then she was gone. The word *disconnected* appeared on the screen, replacing the video transmission.

"Now there's a word," Jordan said to the screen.

The watch on his wrist, a vintage Tramway exchanged between timekeepers, confirmed the time when the night sky faded into light. Jordan grabbed his key to the cottage—the super-programmed iPhone—and walked outside to a familiar stand of trees. There, under the oaks, he recalled the graduation party at Continuum that unfolded on a night much like this one: LouAnn, a blanket by the fire, and the journeys of time that awaited.

Through the fog, he saw a figure in a lawn chair, silhouetted by the lake that glowed silver in the moonlight. With his gaze fixed on the lake, the figure raised his arm and beckoned Jordan to the empty chair next to him. Jordan followed, taking the seat next to the Timekeeper.

Each morning before sunrise, he returned, alone, to the chair by the lake, awaiting a message across the emptiness of time. A voice would come to him in the darkness before dawn. "Where are you, Billy Pilgrim?" LouAnn asked as the half-light of morning turned into the bright promise of the day.

AUTHOR'S NOTE

It has taken time to understand the impact of mass steel mill closings in the US in 1977. Many historians, social scientists, and journalists now believe it was a moment that signaled the end of industrial America and the beginning of the digital age.

The Timekeeper's Daughter unfolds at that time. Based on real events, the principal characters—technologist LouAnn Epperson, her steelmaker father, Lou Epperson, and newspaper reporter, Jordan Maier—transport us through interconnected themes that remain with us today: the mystery of time, the shameful barriers of gender discrimination, the power of transformational technologies, and the reckless public-policy decisions that decimated communities.

The Eppersons and Maier are based on real people who lived in Youngstown, Ohio, at the time. Their lives, however, have been reimagined around an actual event: Black Monday, a day that changed industrial America and impacted hundreds of thousands of people.

I was a reporter in Youngstown at the time. The account of Black Monday in the fictional "Youngstown Examiner" reflects a compilation of coverage at Youngstown's local newspaper, *The Youngstown Vindicator*. Newsroom characters are based on real people there. While scenes and dialogue are fictional, they reflect the culture and conversations in newsrooms at the time. Ironically, *The Youngstown Vindicator* ceased operations in 2019 when *The Timekeeper's Daughter* was being edited.

The conspiracy between the US steel industry and the federal government that is described in the book is also real. It is based on my reporting at *The Vindicator*, including a series called *The Lykes Files* that was published in 1978.

The executives at "Youngstown Steel" and at the US attorney general's office are also based on real people. For the fictionalized accounts, I've attempted to capture their personalities, their speech, their behaviors, and their motivations. Readers, for example, will recognize similarities between the fictional Winston Dell III and Griffin Bell, the attorney general at the time.

As a journalist, I have been asked why I did not take a traditional journalistic approach to recounting the Youngstown story. My best answer is that journalism fails most stories across time. The genre of historical fiction enabled me to explore the unreported nuances of time, place, and people that I understand instinctively, as well as through personal experience.

"People are trapped in history," James Baldwin wrote, "and history is trapped in them." *The Timekeeper's Daughter* intends to break the distance between now and then.

I owe a significant thank you to Mary Peskin. Mary changed the perspective of *The Timekeeper's Daughter*. What started as a one-dimensional reminiscence of life in Youngstown became a quest by a brilliant woman to overcome institutional gender discrimination and to use emerging technology to solve the mystery of her father's death. Mary's accounts of sexual discrimination in patriarchal academia and sexist news-organizations inspired a new hero for the story and for our times—a woman to be reckoned with.

ABOUT THE AUTHOR

Community is at the core of Dale Peskin's career in journalism. He believes that quality journalism strengthens communities and guides citizens to sound decisions about life, work, and governance. *The Timekeeper's Daughter*, his debut novel, brings these values to a literary format that expands the understanding of consequential stories with insightful writing about the human condition.

Dale has been widely honored as media innovator, news executive, editor, and journalist. A pioneer across journalism formats and online media, he has been recognized throughout the news industry as a leader of ideas about change in news and at news organizations.

The Timekeeper's Daughter is based, in part, on his reporting for his hometown newspaper, *The Youngstown Vindicator*, that disclosed mismanagement at Youngstown Sheet & Tube Co. and collusion with the Antitrust Division of the US Justice Department. Initially, more than 5,000 steelworkers lost their jobs at Sheet & Tube's Campbell Works in what was at the time, the largest plant closing in US history. About 60,000 steelworkers would lose their jobs in the economic crisis that followed, a moment viewed as the end of the industrial era.

Dale was among the first journalists to embrace online news. As editor of *The Dallas News* website in 1997, *The Dallas Morning News* became the first major news organization to break a significant, investigative story on the Internet. That decision was hailed by some as a landmark of journalism and criticized by others as cannibalization of the newspaper. Breaking news on websites prior to publication in the newspaper is now a frequent practice.

In 2002, he was hired by US newspaper publishers to lead newspapers into the Internet era as executive director of the think tank New Directions for News. Later, he served in a similar capacity at The Media Center at the American Press Institute with a focus on training publishers and editors for online operations. He later cofounded and served as a principal at We Media, a media consulting and research agency.

Dale is married to Mary Peskin, former design director of New York Times Regional Newspapers and a former associate director of The American Press Institute. They live in Northern Virginia where they are avid golfers, travelers, art collectors, and grandparents.

Section photos by Unsplash

CPSIA information can be obtained
at www.ICGtesting.com
Printed in the USA
BVHW080139210721
612415BV00008B/442